Kate McMahon has spent the past twenty years surfing waves all over the world, and regularly arriving to events late with her hair dripping wet. After watching many of her friends compete on the world surfing tour, she wondered how she too could combine a career with her true love; her butt still hurts from pinching herself after landing the dream job as editor of *SurfGIRL* magazine in 2001. Since then, Kate has edited various preschool, tween, teen and music magazines and lives just 100 steps from the sand at Narrabeen on Sydney's Northern Beaches, where she gets up to mischief with all of her amazing surfer girlfriends.

www.katemcmahonmyword.com

facebook.com/katemcmahonmyword

twitter.com/thekatemcmahon

instagram.com/thebikinicollectivebook

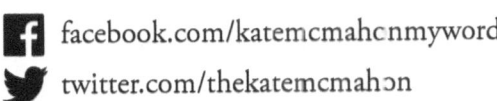

The
Bikini
Collective

Book 2: Lost in LA

Kate McMahon

First published by Kate McMahon in 2019
This edition published in 2019 by Kate McMahon

Copyright © Kate McMahon 2019
www.katemcmahonmyword.com
@thebikinicollectivebook
The moral right of the author has been asserted.

This is a work of fiction. Names, characters, places, organisations and occurrences either are a product of the author's imagination or are used fictitiously. Any resemblance to actual persons, living or dead, or events locales is entirely coincidental.

Lost in LA: The Bikini Collective
ISBN: 978-0-6484782-0-1 PRINT
ISBN: 978-0-6484782-1-8 E-BOOK
The Bikini Collective/Kate McMahon

Cover design and photography by Pepita Wilson
Cover surfing photography by @surfphotosofyou
Cover stars: Jesse and Tru Starling

To the humans I've met on my many travels, thank you for all the experiences and stories shared that make the world a much richer existence. And an extra thanks for those who've shown me their secret surf spots.

#1

Mel crosses the lawn to the clothesline, sniffing the air. She can feel a change coming. Not just a shift to an offshore wind, or the anticipation of a rising swell. Nup, it's something much bigger than that.

She pinches the peg and her cross-back bikinis drop into her hand. Despite being hung out all day, they're still damp. The north coast summer air has created a humidity barrier so thick, not even the sun can penetrate it. She takes a whiff and wrinkles her nose. A mouldy mango would probably smell better.

Walking inside and kicking her bedroom door closed, Mel disconnects her phone from its charger and flops back onto her bed. Still no response from Jaspa. That's so weird. What could be better than surfing out the front at glassy head-high Paradise Point with your best friend?

She leans over and opens the window as far as it will go, and a breeze trickles through the screen, a teasing promise of slight relief. Mel looks over at the itinerary on her desk and googles 'water temperature Los Angeles February'.

What the heck? She types a text.

Holy crapola, did you know it's going to be fifteen freakin' degrees in the water at Malibu? I'm such a gumby in a steamer! Argh!

Mel hates wearing a full wetsuit, it makes her feel suffocated. She usually ends up chopping off the legs or the arms so she can feel the ocean on her skin.

Still no reply from Jaspa. Where the hell is she? They should be surfing. It's the biggest year of their lives.

'Stuff this.' Mel springs up, chucking her phone onto the bed. As she folds her arms through her bikini top she glances at her photo board. In almost every picture, Jaspa's flashing a grin that would melt hearts on impact. Mel, on the other hand, alternates between tongue out, mouth stretched open in a scream, crossed eyes, inverted eyelids, or her signature move: whacking up a subtle middle finger.

She squirts sunscreen into her palm and smears some over her back and shoulder blades, the coconut scent melting into her skin.

She strides up the stairs two at a time, the instant cool from the air-conditioned lounge room tickling over her body as she reaches the top.

'Hey, I'm hitting the point,' she calls through the staircase banister. Her dad's snoozing on the couch while her mum reads a women's magazine with the headline 'Hollywood's Top 10 Trash Bags (and the scandals that gave them the title)' splashed across the cover. Mel teases her mum about her love of gossip mags, but she knows curiosity will get the better of her and she will, eventually, end up reading that list herself.

Her mother removes her reading glasses. 'What time will you be home?' she asks sleepily, rubbing the corner of her eye.

'I've no idea. Depends if it's pumping. Why does it matter?' Mel tightens her grip on the rail, annoyance prickling up her back.

'Well, I need to know when to start dinner, so let's set a time now,' her mum insists through pursed lips.

Mel releases a loud groan that causes her dad to stir. 'What the heck, Mum!' she complains, stomping back down the stairs. 'Why do we always need a schedule?' Being parent-free on the other side of the world can't come soon enough. Only ten and a quarter days to go.

She pauses at the back door, hanging her head with a sigh. Her seven-year-old brother, Daniel, glares at her from the couch, his distraction causing Minecraft's Steve to be set upon by zombies.

'Hey, rugrat,' Mel says sheepishly, hoping he was too enthralled in his virtual world to hear her rant.

'Why are you always such a *bitch* to Mum?' He gives her his best evil-eye glare, then grapples for the remote to reset his game.

Mel sometimes feels bad about the way she bickers with her mother. But seriously, why does she have to make a fuss about every trivial detail? Whose party is it? How will you get there? Where are the parents? What do they do for a living? Who's responsible for everyone's safety? Blah, blah, blah. And spontaneity? Forget about it. When it comes to going with the flow, her mum's a dried-up creek bed. Family holidays are always booked a year in advance, and morning bathroom rosters have to be discussed the night before – even though there are only four of them in the household.

Mel is determined not to turn out like her mother. *Yeah right.* Says the girl who writes herself a daily checklist and has her swimwear categorised in different sections of her drawer according to what surf conditions they cater for.

As she opens the screen door a whoosh of black bounds towards her. She bends down to greet their eight-month-old Labrador-cross-Dachshund, then spies something in its mouth. 'Sausage, you little brat!' Mel takes the leg-rope strap away from the puppy, loops it through her fingers and tucks her surfboard under her arm.

The board almost feels like part of her body. It pinches perfectly under her armpit when she's carrying it, and when she's lying on it in the ocean her hip bones sink into the minor dents they've made over time.

Stepping from her driveway onto the sand, Mel sees waves tunnelling from Paradise Point on her right before fading into an ocean gutter 30 metres from the shore. A build-up of sand has kept the break from achieving peak perfection. Usually you can finish your ride by almost hopping onto the sand. At least, that's what Mel likes to do – usually showing off to whoever happens to be watching.

As Mel makes her way across the beach she spies two familiar figures walking towards her and stops in her tracks. There's a shrub to her right, but it's too small to dart behind. Damn. It was the perfect size when they were seven, playing hide-outs.

Jaspa releases her hand from Cooper's to wave at Mel. If the whole professional surfing thing doesn't work out, Mel could definitely be an actress. She keeps her eyes downcast, pretending not to notice them until the last minute.

'Ah, so that was your BBD,' Mel says playfully, but her shoulders stiffen as Jaspa approaches and wraps her arms around her.

Jaspa lets out an innocent laugh and fidgets with the ends of her wet waist-length hair. 'My what?'

Mel holds her tongue to keep from schooling her best friend on the acronym for 'bigger, better deal' as Cooper cuts in.

'It's more fun out there than it looks, although we could use a cyclone swell to shift that sand,' he says to Mel, squeezing Jaspa into his side and kissing her on the cheek. 'I've gotta head home, Jazz. I'll see you tomorrow, beautiful.'

Mel narrows her eyes as Cooper walks out of earshot. 'So, what, he calls you Jazz now, too?'

'Yeah, it's super cute isn't it?' Jaspa's eyes glisten a deep blue, like they were spawned from the ocean itself, and her lids become heavy. Mel wants to projectile vomit all over them.

'Cute. Yep. That's totally the word I was searching for,' Mel deadpans, but Jaspa smiles anyway. Jaspa's the sweetest person Mel knows, and would never think about chucking inanimate objects at her.

'Well …' Jaspa shifts her weight from foot to foot. 'Guess I'll see you later, then?'

A sneer creeps over Mel's face, a habitual look that's seen her grounded and sent to detention many times. 'Sure, if you can find time in your busy schedule.'

Mel never cringes the actual moment words fall from her mouth. The realisation that she's spoken harshly can take anywhere from five minutes to five months. 'I'll call you after my surf,' she adds without turning around, already halfway down the beach.

As the ocean rushes at Mel's feet, she hops off the protruding rock, landing tummy-first on her surfboard and allowing the water to carry her towards the break. She whips her board around to two-stroke paddle into an oncoming ride, gliding into the pitching lip and springing to her feet. Immediately slicing her surfboard rail into the ocean, Mel speeds to the top of the wave, releases her fins and throws her arms behind her in a layback snap. She starts to race to the next section, but the wave fizzles out as it reaches deeper water. The surfboard sinks beneath her as she stands motionless, staring towards the beach.

Bonita Shores rests in the distance like a lazy old dog who's eaten too much. Clusters of houses are nestled in against the forest. A quaint store that sells everything from fresh bread and groceries to fishing tackle and car parts, along with the Chicken Lickin' takeaway, Treat Yourself ice-creamery and Cuppa cafe, makes up Main Street. From Paradise Point all the way up to the Northies headland, Mel is one of only six people in the water. This is the first time she can remember surfing out the front without Jaspa. She sighs. Is this something she needs to get used to? Being in her hometown feels like trying to squeeze into the rash vest she wore when she was ten.

She can't wait to get out of here.

#2

'Carolyn Fitzgerald, are you ready for the ride of your life?' Mel screams out the window of the mini-van as her friend hands her surfboard bag and backpack to the driver.

Carolyn adjusts her skinny-leg jeans, then climbs up into the van, realising that black and denim could be a terrible combination for a: February and b: thirteen hours on a plane. 'Yo, you know it!' Carolyn strides down the aisle, offering Cooper and Tyler, Jaspa's brother, a quick nod as she passes.

Mel nudges Jaspa's knee with hers and they shuffle over to make room for Carolyn on the back seat.

'Gimme that,' Mel says, snatching Carolyn's passport and flicking through the blank pages. Between them, Mel and Jaspa have been to eight countries, but this is Carolyn's first time overseas. Mel stops at the photo page. 'Ha, brutal. You look like you just caught someone stealing your favourite board.'

'They said not to smile!' Carolyn says, swiping it back from Mel.

Jaspa claps her hands and squeals. 'I'm so excited I could hardly sleep last night.'

'I know,' Mel says without looking up from her phone as she posts a picture of an aeroplane with *Bon voyage, bitches!* as the caption. 'I saw your light on and almost came over so we could be insomnia zombies together.'

After packing her bag, Mel had spent the night zoning out from her parents' lectures about appropriate behaviour while attending her first World Junior Tour event with the Australian surfing team. She'd nodded insincerely, knowing she'd soon be in Los Angeles for one glorious week, free from parental eyes.

The van stops in front of a fibro house that's half hidden by overgrown yucca plants. Wil Sanders and Vijay Kumar climb into the van, making a beeline for the back. 'Alright chicks, thanks for warming the seat for us.' Wil stands in front of the girls with his hands shoved in his pockets, flicking his head in the direction of the row of seats behind the driver.

Jaspa goes to stand up, but Mel yanks her back

down. 'Err, I do not think so.' Mel's eyes meet Wil's and she fixes him with a steely gaze.

'C'mon, you know the drill,' Wil continues, with V-jay waiting timidly behind him. 'You're the new girls on tour, you've gotta earn your status.'

'Leave them alone,' Cooper says, while Tyler slumps down in the seat beside him.

Mel stands up and snaps at Cooper. 'Thanks, but we don't need you to rescue us.' She turns to Wil, her sharp green eyes shadow, warning of a foul mood incoming. 'Do you want a spoon so you can eat those words, William? Last time I looked we,' she points at Jaspa, then Carolyn, then herself, 'are higher on our rankings than you are on yours.' With a cocked hip, she licks her finger and strokes it in the air, giving a point to herself. From behind her, Jaspa snickers quietly while Carolyn snorts.

Thomas Sampson swings around from the front seat, offering his best scowl, which looks kind of like a dolphin trying to be angry. 'Alright, sit the heck down.' A strand of his hair keeps falling over his eye, despite his efforts to push it away. 'We haven't even left the country yet, and I will not hesitate to boot you back home if you don't behave.' He turns back around, masking a smile.

Thomas is the head surf coach at the Institute of Sporting Excellence. The last time Mel heard him come close to shouting was when she got busted ditching surf theory to go surfing. Her protest of 'practice makes perfect' was met with a frustrated sigh and a week's worth of yard clean-up.

Mel recoils, knowing their teacher's not easily rattled. 'Ol' Thommo's got some fire in him after all,' she murmurs to her friends, while smugly telling herself it's obvious Wil still has a soft spot for her. Their quick pash and dash to fulfil a dare at the last elite training weekend clearly meant something more to Wil. But as far as this trip is concerned, Wil remains firmly on Mel's maybe-if-I'm-bored pile.

Signs point them to international departures at Brisbane Airport. Everyone exits the van as their boards and bags are loaded onto a trolley and Thomas helps the team check in.

Mel dances on the spot when they receive their boarding passes.

'Yew, we're all sitting next to each other!' She sees Cooper offer Jaspa a half shrug and wonders if her best friend would rather be elsewhere. Surely not? Jaspa's boyfriend better get used to it – he might've hijacked her over the summer, but this is a chicks' trip, and anyone standing in the way of that better prepare to be mowed down.

Truth is, the blame falls partly on Mel. After all, it

was Mel who rounded Jaspa and Cooper together like a cattle-dog cupid. The sparks between them were brighter than Sydney Harbour on New Year's Eve and Mel couldn't bear to see Jaspa's doe-eyes any longer when it was so clear Cooper was into her. But lately Mel's found herself getting caught in the firing line between Jaspa and Cooper's exchanges. A wink here, a gooey smile there. Eww.

The worst thing is, Jaspa going off with Cooper has left Mel alone with her thoughts, and this journey of self-discovery has her unravelling at a rapid rate, leaving her increasingly agitated and dissatisfied. In their friendship, Mel has always been in the driver's seat, but with Jaspa increasingly unavailable, Mel was starting to see herself as a third wheel. At home, Mel felt a sudden urgent need for freedom from her parents' curfews and constraints, which seemed so absurd. And suddenly, Bonita Shores' population of 1800 just seemed so *ordinary*.

An audible sigh escapes Mel's lips as she looks at Jaspa and Carolyn, seated beside her. It's already been over an hour since take-off.

'Hey sleepy, we thought you'd dozed off already.'

Jaspa ushers Mel closer and holds her phone up. 'Come on, we haven't even taken a selfie yet.'

Mel grins, leans into Jaspa's shoulder, sticks her tongue out the side of her mouth and flashes her middle finger.

'There,' Jaspa says, placing her phone in the seat pocket in front of her. 'The road – or should I say, plane – trip has officially begun!'

Mel's stomach does a flip. She's on her way to Malibu. In California. Right next to Hollywood. If there's anywhere to take her life beyond the mediocre, it's there. 'I've got an idea. Jaspa, do you have your notebook?' Mel snatches it from Jaspa, and flips past her journal entries to a fresh page. 'Can we write here?'

'Sure,' Jaspa shrugs. 'What are we doing?'

'Well,' Mel starts scrawling. 'Let's make a manifestation list of all the things we want to happen on this journey. Carolyn, you first.'

'Win the comp.'

'Ha, nice one!' Mel scrawls, then looks up. 'Jaspa?'

'We can't all win the event, so maybe just to surf our best?'

'Done. What else?'

'I wanna skate at Venice Beach.'

'Carolyn wants to rollerblade at Venice …' Mel says aloud with a smirk while pretending to write. Carolyn jabs her in the ribs and she buckles over with a cackle, then writes, *skateboarding at Venice Beach*.

'Window shopping along Santa Monica Boulevard. And waffles afterwards,' Jaspa adds.

'My goal ...' Mel begins, 'apart from surfing of course, is to meet someone brilliant and famous, like Liam Hemsworth or something.'

'Dude, he's always in Byron Bay.' Carolyn rips open the packet of nuts handed out by the flight attendant. 'I've dropped in on him heaps of times.'

Mel cocks her head in protest. 'You know what I mean. Just someone *exciting*.' She closes her eyes with a wide grin and cranks back her seat. 'Someone who's done something *cool* with their lives.'

Yep, this is it. This is the trip that will change everything, Mel can feel it.

#3

Mel stops abruptly. 'Are you freakin' kidding me?' she says with a gaping mouth. 'Surely we've got the wrong address?'

Jaspa follows Mel through the front door, puts down her suitcase and draws in a long breath. 'Oh. My. God.'

'Where's Carolyn?' Mel demands, looking over her shoulder. 'Carolyn, get your hot ass over here and feast your eyeballs, my friend.'

Mel kicks off her white Vans and walks down the hallway over the speckled grey marble floor, passing a row of framed vintage surf photos mounted on the wall. Jumping the two steps leading down to the sunken living room, she reaches the floor-to-ceiling glass windows and yanks open the sliding doors.

Thomas follows her out onto the deck. 'Not bad, eh?' he smirks.

'Understatement alert.' She peers over the elevated infinity pool to see the ocean lapping almost up to the sandbags wedged against the exterior of the house. 'You told us it was a beach shack, not a beach *mansion*! Are we trespassing right now, Thommo?'

He rolls his eyes and shakes his head. 'Firstly, that's Mr Sampson to you. And, no, it belongs to an old friend of mine who's letting us rent it at mates rates for the week.'

'Oi, wait til you see our room,' Carolyn yells down from the upstairs balcony. 'It's next-level sickness.'

Mel leaps from the side of the pool and runs up the spiral staircase and into the bedroom, where Jaspa and Carolyn are on the balcony sitting in a hammock. 'Is this just for us?' she asks, spying the three single beds.

'Yep!' Jaspa lightly claps her hands. 'The other girls are all in the bigger room with a TV, but we get the ocean view.'

Mel leans over the railing and sees Cooper and Tyler take a running jump and dive-bomb into the pool. 'Is it cold?' she calls to them.

'Nah, it's heated,' Cooper yells back before blowing a kiss up at Jaspa.

Mel responds by sticking her finger in her throat.

'This pad is so quirky,' she says, squeezing onto the hammock with her friends to take in their new backyard.

An old wooden rowboat has been converted into an outdoor lounge and piled with blue-and-white-striped pillows and red blankets. There are lifesaver rings nailed to the fence, and thick woven sailing ropes hold up hanging plant pots. An old anchor is mounted on the side of an outdoor shower with two towels hanging from the dips. Mel appreciates the nautical theme, but if this was her house she would make it total glam. For starters, the pool would be surrounded by black diamond-encrusted tiles, there'd be an elevated DJ plat-form in the middle decked out with strobe lights, and a zip-line down from the balcony. The outdoor couches would be in the shape of lips and the interior of the house would be all white, with splashes of red and leopard print. The entrance hall would feature a Wall of Fame where all the Hollywood celebrities who visited her would leave a message: *Mel's a star*, etc.

Carolyn bounces in the hammock. 'Raaa, I get to live on the beach for a whole freakin' week!'

Mel tickles Carolyn's ribs. While she and Jaspa already have homes with an ocean view, Carolyn lives with her mum in a tiny two-bedroom unit at Pacific Grove. That's probably why she's forever hitchhiking to stay with Mel or Jaspa at Bonita Shores. Mel doesn't really see the appeal. Apart from the surf, there's zero to do. At least in Pacific Grove there are shops, organic cafes, house parties, music festivals – Carolyn should be *grateful*.

'Holy heck, you'll never guess what I can see.' Mel kneels on the couch at the far end of the balcony and stares out to sea, the corners of her mouth upturned. Jaspa and Carolyn run over and flop down beside her. 'Look, it's Malibu point!'

Mel's been desperate to visit this wave since seeing it on the video for 'Life is Swell' by Double Denim – a Santa Monica all-girl band she became obsessed with last year. It's not because it's one of the most famous right-handers in the world – her home break would rival it. No, when Mel thinks about Malibu it's all sunny Californian beach party vibes, where you never know which famous person you might be sharing the sand with. At Bonita Shores the most exciting thing that's happened lately is the surf lifesaving club adding a lame-ass weekly youth yoga and meditation session. Honestly, why would she want to waste an hour of her life thinking about *nothing*? Here, at Malibu, anything can happen.

Lines of swell wander in from the horizon, wrapping onto the rocks and creating a long wall of water that breaks south away from the house towards a jetty. At least three surfers, mainly on longboards, share each ride, trimming along the top and cutting back into each other. 'Life is Swell' gets stuck in Mel's head.

> *'If you wanna ride that's fine by me*
> *on the pavement or out to sea*
> *but hear this boy, make no mistake*
> *I'll leave you frothing in my wake.'*

She jumps to her feet, singing aloud, feeling a sudden urgency to get amongst it. 'Hey Thommo. Oops, I mean *Mr Sampson*,' she calls from over the balcony. 'Can we use those Mals?'

Thomas looks at the rack of boards along the back fence. 'Yes. But bring them back in one piece please, and be back before our 5 pm meeting.'

Mel gives Thomas the thumbs-up, then turns to Jaspa and Carolyn. 'Let's take out the longboards?'

Jaspa stifles a laugh. 'What happened to your rule of always practising on the board you'll use in competition?'

'I know, I know.' Mel holds up her arms with her wrists together. 'Cuff me now, guilty as charged. But we can't *not* ride a Malibu – it's Malibu!'

'I get dibs on the lightning bolt one, suckers,'

Carolyn says as she springs up and sprints down the stairs before they have a chance to protest.

The three boards clunk clumsily together as the girls descend the steps onto the sand.

'Shortboards are so much easier,' Mel says, hoisting 9 feet of bright purple fibreglass onto her head. She tries to imagine what it was like back in the day before legropes. A carnage of abandoned longboards in the shore break, all smashing into each other.

They reach the Malibu lagoon and wade into the ocean towards a cluster of rocks that other surfers paddle out from. Someone catches Mel's eye. He strides through the shallows, the water wetting his skinny-legged black jeans, which are so tight he can barely roll them up above his ankles. A black leather jacket is slung over his shoulder, his slim build clearly defined under a tight blue T-shirt with barely any skin showing between his tattoos. Mel can't see under his oversized Valley sunglasses, but she's sure he smiled in her direction. She cocks a hip to the side, suddenly glad Carolyn talked her into buying a wetsuit jacket to wear over her steamer. He must've noticed how rock'n'roll she looks.

'Oi, are you coming or what?' Carolyn stops paddling, looking back towards the beach. Jaspa is already positioned out the back.

Mel turns from the shore, waves a hand and

launches her board into the ocean, gliding onto her stomach. Each stroke propels her over the breaking water, the nose of the board rising high then smashing down with a thud. Not long after Mel reaches the line-up a wave comes directly to her. Straddling the board, she yanks it around and soars easily into the ride, popping straight to her feet. A friendly line of blue beckons her along and she stylishly walks back and forth along the board, her unzipped jacket blowing in the breeze. The cool afternoon air tickles Mel's cheeks, and the wave keeps unravelling before her, with no threat of bucking her off.

Jaspa and Carolyn look back towards Mel from down the line and begin stroking into her ride. 'Yes, go, go!' she screams, stalling the board to give them room. They drop in and clumsily avoid smashing into each other, crouching low to regain control, the fins of their boards slicing through the steely blue. An end section forms on a shallow bank and they're forced to straighten out towards the beach in fits of giggles.

'Look at all those ridiculous houses.' Mel points at the mansions dotted along the shoreline, stretching back up into the mountains. 'I wonder who lives there?'

Carolyn snorts. 'Obviously peeps who aren't counting their pennies.'

'I think those places would get kinda lonely,' Jaspa

says as they unleash their leg-ropes and begin the 300 metre walk back to paddle out.

'Nah, you wouldn't be alone.' Mel kicks the sand with her toes. 'Imagine all the people who'd want to be your friend.' Her mind wanders back to the guy on the beach. *Who is he?* She resolves to find out.

#4

'C'mon, rise and shine.' Mel whips the doona from Jaspa's body and drops it on the floor, then walks over to Carolyn's bed and does the same to her. 'Thommo says we've gotta be downstairs in ten for breakfast.'

Jaspa shivers. 'I honestly didn't expect it to be this chilly.' She leans over the bed to reach for the doona, but Mel kicks it away.

'Nu-uh. Let's go, princess. It'll be toasty as soon as the sun's out.'

On the way downstairs, Mel passes Pepita Mapstone in the hallway. A satin eye mask is pushed on top of her head, her jet-black fringe spiking out at the sides. Her matching Victoria's Secret gingham pyjamas are twisted at the waist.

'Remind me why we're up so early. This is an outrageous hour.' Pepita struggles to look through half-shut eyes and fumbles for the bathroom doorknob.

'Ha, ain't it true,' Mel chirps without stopping to chat. Mel doesn't know the other girls on the Australian team very well. She only met Pepita last year at the final qualifying event, and even then she wasn't in the mindset for making new friends. She offers her emotions sparingly, not wanting to risk them getting in the way of the things that need to get done.

Down in the kitchen, Mel lifts the lid off the pot simmering on the stove. She scoops berry porridge into her bowl, then slides into the seat next to Tyler. 'So,' she says, spooning a heap of hot oats into her mouth and talking through the stickiness, 'you're competing this year after all? Looks like your graciousness was short-lived.' Mel's not one to shy away from telling it like it is. After failing to qualify for the World Junior Tour, Tyler went into meltdown, having a dummy spit at the contest site and later ending up lost at sea after attempting to surf in wild conditions. Most of this stemmed from his jealousy of his sister's success. After his rescue, and much time for reflection, Tyler had promised to chaperone Jaspa during her first year on tour. That is, until a late withdrawal by another competitor saw him next in line and faced with an important decision.

'Wow.' Tyler pulls back and crinkles his brow. 'Harsh.' He hunches over his breakfast bowl and continues shovelling food in. 'You would've done the same, Appleby.'

'Damn straight. Jaspa wouldn't have though.'

'She'll be right. Cooper won't let her outta his sight,' Tyler says, clearly intending to stir up trouble.

Mel bristles, and doesn't even attempt to hide her sneer. 'We'll see about that.' She stares down Tyler's smirk. There's no way she's going to let her best friend become dependent on a guy. Mel's mum is a shining example of how life looks under the thumb. Mel hates the way her dad throws snide remarks when her mum expresses an opinion that challenges his. 'Silly woman' is his go-to term. Or the scolding she cops when something's slipped off the shopping list – honestly, get your own freakin' Tim Tams, seriously.

'See about what?' Jaspa asks innocently, arriving at the table.

'See about us dominating our first heat today. Now sit your ass here and let's talk strategy.' Mel pulls out a chair for Jaspa and flips her middle finger at Tyler while Jaspa's not looking. She kicks out the chair on her other side. 'Carolyn. Come.' Mel places a knife on the table and covers half of it with a crumpled-up napkin.

'Now, *chicas*, remember with point breaks we have to stay in the pocket of the wave.' Mel taps the napkin serving as the wave's whitewater.

'That's a serviette, not a pocket,' says Carolyn, straight-faced.

'I'll do the jokes, thanks. Now focus.' Mel rips off a corner of toast and manoeuvres it between the napkin and the knife. 'What Jaspa and I will have to avoid is being too far out on the face, too many cutties. Jazz, we need to mix up the styles of our top turns. Carolyn, you're on your backhand, so just point as vert as you can go and crank that spray like a ninja.'

'I can't believe we get to surf Malibu with just three others.' Jaspa jiggles her arms in a little dance.

'I know, right?' Mel licks her spoon and points it at Jaspa. '*And* we get to beat 'em.' She laughs at Jaspa's eye roll. Like her friend, Mel is definitely in it for the fun, but *coming first* is fun. In fact, for her it's the most fun. Mel did her Year 9 history assignment on her favourite sporting victories. She titled the project *Winning*. Cathy Freeman's 2000 Olympic medal came in a close second – she still gets goosebumps watching that clip – but it was surfer Trudy Hardwick's first world title victory that she placed on the top of her list. Trudy had to retrieve her board from the rocks at Maui after snapping her leg-rope, then immediately went on to score a ten-point ride after requiring a nine-eight with only five minutes left. Mel had bitten almost every nail down to the cuticle as she watched on with the rest of her class – one of many perks of attending a school that specialises in sport.

'Alrighty, listen up you lot,' Thomas says as he walks into the kitchen. He draws in a deep breath and holds it, which he always does before making any announcement, as though he has to prepare his otherwise jovial self for serious or important conversations. 'Round one of the girls will surf today. Carolyn, you're heat three, Jaspa five and Mel six. I've told the others to meet us outside at the pool in thirty minutes. We'll walk down together.'

Tyler places his dish in the sink and turns to walk upstairs. 'When are they running the guys?'

'Later in the week – there's meant to be a new swell coming. And do your dishes you lot, I'm not gonna be your butler this week,' Thomas adds.

'Typical,' Mel mumbles to Jaspa and Carolyn as she grabs their dirty bowls. 'Of course the guys get to surf when there's more swell. I might write a post about that for our page.'

Mel thinks back to the letter of complaint they

wrote to surfing magazine *Salt Action* last year, criti-
cising the lack of female representation, other than
sexist images, which they signed off as 'The Bikini
Collective' to celebrate the empowerment of women in
sport. The post received thousands of shares and likes,
and Mel, Jaspa and Carolyn morphed The Bikini
Collective into a closed online support group for surfer
girls to share stories and tips, ask questions, seek advice
and generally create a community.

'Great idea!' Jaspa says, wiping the dishes as Mel
hands them to her. 'We haven't uploaded anything since
we've been here. I could even help with research or facts
or something.'

'Oh hell yeah. I usually want to scratch your eyes
out for being gorgeous *and* smart, but I need you right
now. C'mon, let's talk about this while we get ready,'
Mel says, ushering Jaspa and Carolyn upstairs.

Jaspa sits on her bed to screw fins into her surfboard. 'What about some kind of comparison, like the
number of times men have competed in better conditions than the women over the past year?'

'It's getting heaps better than it used to be,' Carolyn
says, rolling up her wetsuit and shoving it into her backpack. 'Well, that's what my boss says, anywayz.'
Working in a surf shop that's owned by an ex-profes-
sional female surfer means Carolyn gets more than just

a pay cheque each week. During lunchbreaks or quiet periods, she's schooled on everything from the lack of sponsorship for women's surfing in the '80s and '90s, through to how the boom in chick's surfwear began.

Mel stands in the doorway of the en suite wiping toothpaste from her mouth with a towel. 'Better's fine, but it's gotta be betterer than better.'

'Betterer? I love it when you make up words,' Jaspa giggles.

'I know,' Mel says, hopping on the bed and standing with her arms outstretched. 'I'm the world's most unrecognised literary genius. I'm going to start a dictionary and call it a fictionary.'

'Girls.' They halt, waiting for Thomas' breath-drawn pause. 'Down in five, please.'

Mel hops from the bed, wrestles her arms through the straps in her backpack and picks up her surfboard. 'Aren't you just so impressed with Thommo's level of authoritar on this trip? And shut your face up,' Mel says, pointing at Jaspa with a smirk as they head downstairs. 'It is a word.'

'What time period do you want me to look at for the story?' Jaspa asks as they descend the steps onto the beach. The high tide laps right up to the house, so they need to wait for an outgoing wave before they can jump down and run along to more exposed sand.

'Whoa, that's gnarly,' Mel gasps as she reaches higher ground. 'I wonder what it's like on a big swell! Righto, why don't we try to compare the past, say, five or ten years?'

'I could bung it into an illo,' Carolyn says. While academia isn't her strength, she's celebrated around town for her incredible street art. Well, at least for her *legal* street art. What they don't know about her Mz Grip graf tag won't hurt them.

'Oh my god, a frickin' info graphic, yes! You know how much I love a pie chart. But let's do it all when we get back to Australia. Right now we're in Cali-freakin'-fornia and there's too much fun to be had.' Mel kicks out of her thongs to squeak barefoot across the sand. Jesus! Look at that set-up. It's like an entire festival.' Scaffolding that's almost the size of their Malibu mansion sits on the sand in front of the car park and is covered in sponsors' banners. Rows of umbrellas and sun lounges are lined right up to the high-tide shoreline for spectators to claim a front-row view. A stage is wedged between two sets of speakers. 'Thommo.' Mel catches his sigh and raised eyebrows. 'Soz, habit. *Mr Sampson.* Are all the junior events this pimp?'

He shakes his head. 'Only the ones preceding another contest. There's a six-star WQS here next week.'

That's Mel's two-year plan. Gather enough experience in the junior events and then hit the World Qualifying Series. Another two years there and she should make the main world tour by the time she's twenty, and world champion by twenty-four.

They climb the stairs to the surfers' area. There's a rack for their boards, lockers for their belongings, a waiter serving free coffee *and* chai tea (Jaspa will be stoked), a buffet of fruit and pastries (Carolyn will be stoked), tables with USB ports, four televisions showing the contest's live broadcast, and an entire area full of hammocks. Mel slots her board into the rack, drops her bag on the floor and does a 360 degree turn to take it all in.

'Hey girls,' interrupts a voice behind them. 'Aren't you the three from Pacific Grove who started The Bikini Collective?'

Mel can't believe that three-time world champion Trudy Hardwick is standing in front of them – and she knows who *they* are! This is the woman who, when the world tour announced that Teahupo'o in Tahiti was too dangerous to include on the women's tour, flew straight over during the men's event to free surf waves you could fit a double-storey house inside. This is the woman who refused to pose for America's *Surf Scape* magazine when she won her third world title because they wanted to run a portrait image instead of a surf shot.

It's not often Mel is lost for words but she's struggling now. 'No. I mean, yes. Well, Carolyn's from Pacific Grove and Jazz and I are from Bonita Shores. I can't believe you know about The Bikini Collective, that's a little bit awesome.' She giggles like a groupie. *For god's sake, girl, get a grip!*

Trudy smiles warmly. Her body is strong, the upper half broad then narrowing into a tiny waist hugged by a tight-fitting hoodie, and her face is naturally tanned with a smothering of freckles that seem to celebrate a life of outdoors. 'It was a really important conversation you started, and there are so many more to have.' She swoops her arm behind the three of them and points towards the table. 'Here, do you have time to talk for a minute?'

Mel turns wide-eyed to Jaspa and Carolyn. *Is this even happening?* They nod, and follow Trudy to the table.

'I'm here for a meeting with one of my sponsors, and when I saw your names on the contest heat draw …'

Wait, she *looked* for their names? Holy crap!

'… I thought we could do some kind of mentoring session while we're here.'

Heck yes. This is what Mel's all about, filling young girls with inspiration. She reverts to her serious voice, the one that she hopes will one day see her become the spokeswoman for surfing. 'That would be incredible. We can post it on our socials for whoever's in the area.'

'Yes!' Jaspa claps her hands lightly, like a child who's been promised sweets. 'Should we do a learn-to-surf day?'

'Absolutely,' Trudy says. 'I can arrange all the equipment and instructors through the local surf school.'

'But let's make it more than that.' Mel unzips her jacket and slips it onto the back of the chair. 'What about a panel of surfers, talking about competing and life on tour?'

'Too easy,' Trudy grins. 'I can ask around to see who's here.'

Carolyn pulls off her cap and flips it on backwards. 'I ain't doing the panel thing though. You know I hate that stuff.'

'No worries, Carolyn.' Mel always makes it her mission to help her friends overcome their insecurities. 'You can contribute another way. Umm, what about a surf art workshop?'

'Oh yeah, that's hell good, I can do that.'

Jaspa grabs Carolyn's arm. 'I know! I'll write out some inspirational quotes and each girl can choose which ones they want to sketch.' Jaspa is obsessed with quotes. It's her role to pretty them up and place them over pictures on The Bikini Collective's Instagram page.

Mel bites her bottom lip and nods to herself with a grin. This is gonna be sick. They've only been in LA one night and already it feels like they're making their mark.

#5

The morning sun penetrates Mel's wetsuit, sending a ripple of warmth tickling up her back. Sprawled on the sand with her legs spread wide, Mel leans forward and folds into a deep stretch, the muscles in her back loosening as she takes each extension that little bit further. She raises her eyes to spot Jaspa on another wave, guessing it must be her fifth ride this heat. Malibu suits her style. She flows between her turns with no aggression or rigidness, but unleashes power the moment the wave steepens. Over the roar of the ocean, Mel hears a commentator announce that Jaspa needs a 4.5 to move into second place and an 8.8 for first. Mel draws '7.9' in the sand, then smirks when Jaspa's score is announced as 7.5. Close enough. She'd never make a good judge on tour, unless of course overscoring your best friend is allowed.

As the green board comes down from the judges' tower the yellow board goes up to indicate there are five minutes remaining in Jaspa's heat, meaning Mel can paddle into position for hers. She hops onto sand patches that break up the cluster of rocks and sucks in her breath as her feet fully submerge into the cold water.

'Holy freakin' hell, what the f–,' Mel says through clenched teeth, letting out a groan at the last word. She hears something behind her and swings around.

Mel recognises the girl. It's Gloria Cruz. She's already been on the junior circuit for two years and now also competes in the qualifying events on the world tour. It's the hair that gives it away. Mel saw the Instagram story of her shaving her head, the strands of coal-black locks falling to the floor as love heart emojis flooded phone screens. The undercut is as spectacular in person as it is online. It's only on the right side and wraps around the back of her head, so her hair swoops over to the left.

'I thought they bred 'em tougher where you're from,' Gloria says. Her stance is strong and her face holds an expression that could definitely be mistaken for being pissed off. Or perhaps she is pissed. Perhaps this is her game plan.

Mel continues to wade up to her waist. 'We're tough when it comes to snakes and spiders,' Mel laughs, pausing to push her board over a breaking wave, 'but not when it comes to jumping into a bucket of ice. I'm sure it was warmer yesterday, wasn't it?'

'Yeah. It's the cold currents,' Gloria says with a penetrating stare. Her dark eyes storm under heavy lids, and her thick brows dip at the centre.

Mel spies the other two competitors close behind them. 'See you out there,' she says to Gloria, hopping on her board and duckdiving through the impact zone. *That was really weird,* Mel thinks to herself, pondering why Gloria's so guarded.

Once Mel gets past the whitewater, she sits upright on her board. Her right foot cramps, so she yanks it onto the deck to loosen the leg-rope, then flexes her toes. The ocean is calm for the first 10 minutes of the heat, then a line of waves march in from the horizon. Mel strokes to get on the inside of her competitors and swings quickly to take the first wave of the set. She rides high along the face and rocks her feet to generate speed, but the water folds over a rock and shuts down in front of her. Flicking her board from under her feet, she covers her head with her arms and rolls with the foam. As she pops up, she sees the same thing happen to the girls in pink and yellow vests. Gloria, however, is positioned 30 feet further down the point and paddles into a perfectly formed wave. Mel grits her teeth and makes a beeline for the same take-off position while watching Gloria speed towards the Malibu jetty as spray from each of her turns lingers in the air.

Man, she's good, Mel thinks as she looks back out to sea and patters her hands impatiently on the water. Better than any junior Mel's seen back home. She shakes the doubt from her shoulders as a wave angles towards her, the pitching lip an open invitation to hop on. With two easy strokes she's up. She carves a deep bottom turn then wraps her board into the top pocket of foam. As she races further ahead she realises the wave becomes sluggish if you're too far out on the face. A cutback doesn't have high scoring potential but she's got no choice, she needs to get back to where the power of the wave is. Her ride ends and she pushes off the sand to paddle back into position. She sighs in frustration. The score will be okay, enough to push her into second place, but she needs to get a better read on Malibu. Her surfing is zippy, which just feels awkward under a slow-moving wall of water.

Gloria glides into her fourth wave and weaves along the head-high stretch of blue. *How does she do it?* She's not having any trouble generating speed. As Mel continues her paddle up the point, Gloria stomps on her back foot and releases her fins to send a spray in Mel's direction. Mel tucks her head behind her arm to avoid a soaking, then pulls each hand through the ocean to propel herself forward. The first wave of the set she kicks into doesn't break until closer to shore and she misses it. Mel smacks her fist against the sea.

Dammit.

She wrenches her board around and sees that she's in position for the next one. The lip picks her up and gives her a gentle push, which she uses to soar up the wave, throwing her whole upper body into a top turn.

Now that's more like it.

Her feet swivel against the wax to slice the rail of her board through the water, over and over until she's almost at the shore. Screams unleash from the crowd, and Mel grins, knowing they must be coming from Jaspa and Carolyn.

When Mel doesn't ride a wave well, she feels awkward, like she doesn't belong. But when her turns are perfectly timed, she can't imagine being anywhere else. It's all about finding her place.

The siren sounds and Mel glances at Gloria, offering her a smile as they catch the whitewater in on their bellies.

'Nice one,' is all Gloria says with a steely gaze.

Wait, Mel thinks. Does she mean, 'Nice one, that

was a great wave – sure, you came second but you surfed really well'? Or 'Nice one, bitch, don't even think about trying to beat me again'?

For the first time in Mel's life, she thinks she needs to get a better read on people.

#6

'Yippee, we're all through to round two!' Jaspa throws her arms around Mel as she comes in from her heat, not caring that Mel's wet rash vest is soaking her shirt.

'I know, it's freakin' mad,' Mel mumbles. 'But you do realise your boobs are suffocating me?'

'Yo, those things are lethal,' Carolyn says, pushing Mel further into Jaspa's chest.

Mel bites her bottom lip and grabs Carolyn in a headlock, pulling her close as they all collapse on the sand in titters.

Gloria stops short and then swerves as the three girls almost fall into her.

'She looks friendly,' Carolyn deadpans, wriggling out from Mel's grip.

Mel leans on her knees to steady her breath. 'Oh

yeah, she's real pleasant, a real barrel of laughs, that one.'

'She is?' Jaspa asks.

Mel notices the half-smile Jaspa uses when she pretends to get a gag that's actually soared over her head. 'I'm *joking*, Jazz. She's a total weirdo. Like, she doesn't move her mouth when she speaks.' Mel mimics her last sentence through closed lips.

'She rips, but,' Carolyn says, grabbing Mel's surfboard so she can pull off the competition vest.

'That she does.' Mel gestures to the volunteer at the check-in table and throws her the rashie with a grin. 'Good catch, thanks little legend.' She turns and walks with the girls up to the contest platform. 'You should see her surf up close, it's off the hook.'

'See who surf?'

'Gloria, Jaspa. Focus, focus!' Mel wonders how she can feel such equal measures of love and annoyance for her best friend. Mel calls her the academic ditz. Jaspa could be acing an A+ in an exam, then trip over nothing at all while leaving the classroom. Or she might school you on the biology of the local marine life, but without fail she loses her phone at least once a year. Strangers often mistake them for sisters because of the way Mel snaps back.

'Watch it, Jazz!' She grabs Jaspa's arm, yanking her

aside to avoid a waitress who's struggling to carry a large pot to the competitors' platform. 'I will not hesitate to point my finger at you if a hundred surfers go hungry.'

'Hold up, we even get fed *lunch*?' Carolyn's jaw drops and she widens her eyes.

'You seriously should be the pin-up girl for buffets.' Mel jabs Carolyn in the ribs as they bound up the stairs.

'So what?' Carolyn flinches and sharpens her tone. 'Gotta get it while you can.'

Mel glances sideways at Jaspa and offers an awkward smile. Sometimes she forgets that something like going out for a smashed avocado and latte brunch is a once-in-four-month occasion for Carolyn. Not that Carolyn would be caught dead sipping a latte.

The steam from the tray of hot vegetable curry tickles Mel's nostrils as she piles a big spoonful onto her rice. The three girls place their plates on the chest-high table and pull their stools close together so they can all see the ocean.

'Who's surfing now?' Jaspa asks, while spitting into a tissue and mopping up the splatter of curry she'd spilt on her top.

Mel turns to look back at the television screen. 'Oh, this'll be interesting. Pepita and Tara are in the same heat. Bags not sitting between them at dinner tonight if one of them loses.'

'Who do you want to win?' Carolyn has a way of subtly provoking debate – unlike Mel, who grabs that stick and relentlessly pokes the bear.

'Ummm, I quite like Tara.' Jaspa wriggles her finger at Mel. 'I know you tease her for being a bogan, but she's actually really sweet.'

'Hey,' Mel drops her fork and holds up her hands in protest. 'I love a boag. Who am I to question the plural of you as youse, or the functionality of wearing socks with thongs?' Mel blurts a single laugh at her joke, then says matter-of-factly, 'I actually want Pepita to win.'

'Why? I think Tara's better, she's got more guts,' Carolyn says, breaking apart a bread roll.

Mel stuffs a spoonful of rice into her mouth. 'Because,' she chews, then swallows, 'it would add a bit of diversity to Australian surfing. We can't all be whities, that's boring.'

'Err, I ain't exactly white,' Carolyn says, stroking the side of her face.

Mel pinches Carolyn's cheeks. 'No you're not, you're my little mochaccino.' Realising she should have given more thought to the conversation, as usual Mel decides to make light of it. Carolyn doesn't know who her father is, and any attempt to get the details out of her mother ends up with her sobbing that it was just one night, and can't they just move forward and forget?

Carolyn manages to forget most of the time, except sometimes – like now, when she's looking at the colour of her skin.

'But if we're to compare the two – Pepita and Tara,' Mel continues, 'Pep's Asian and a wicked drummer, does pretty sick airs, and posts heaps of stuff about women's rights. I just think she's an awesome role model. Almost as good as me,' she smirks.

Mel presses a finger to her lips as the commentator bellows over the speakers. 'Pepita Mapstone, your last ride scored a 6.8. That puts you in third place, requiring a 5.5 to push you into second. There are ten minutes remaining.'

Mel drums her hands on the table. 'Yew, go Pep!'

'Go Tara!' Carolyn teases back, throwing her voice to the air.

'Good to see you're all supporting each other,' Thomas interrupts, leaning his forearms on the balcony railing. 'Well done, you all got through to round two.' He pulls his phone out of his pocket and scrolls through his calendar. 'We'll meet back at the house in two hours to watch back over your heats and debrief, okay?'

'Roger that,' Mel says as Thomas walks away to greet a woman who's seated on the other side of the deck. Her silky cream button-up shirt is neatly tucked into khaki slacks that stop at the ankle, and layers of long hair frame her oversized sunglasses. At first glance she looks completely out of place, but people are buzzing around her, either getting her coffee, stopping to talk or waving at her across the room.

'I wonder who she is?' Mel nods towards the woman. 'If Thommo is trying to have a crack then we definitely need to give him a makeover or he has zero chance. First the dad jeans need to go – the whole baggy from crotch to feet thing he's got goin' on is not pretty.'

'She looks quite, like, classy, don't you think?' Jaspa unravels her legs from the stool and peers over the table at Mel. 'What are you doing?'

'Shhhh.' Mel leans her phone upright on the table and subtly looks down at the screen to click the camera. She crops the photo so it's just the woman's face, then looks up at Jaspa and Carolyn. 'Let's have a little Google reverse image snoop, shall we? Oh, no way, look.' The girls lean in and Mel scrolls up the screen. 'She's the bloody boss of the whole world tour.'

'Ah, it's the A-Team,' a voice interrupts. 'You all made it through, that's awesome.' Cooper stands behind Jaspa, places his hands on her shoulders and bends down to kiss her cheek. She looks up and nuzzles her nose into the crook of his neck, closing her eyes to breathe in the ocean scent crusted on his skin.

Mel watches Cooper stroke Jaspa's hair, running his

fingers to the tips and then back up, scooping her mane into a ponytail and massaging her neck. She imagines how it would feel to have a boy not be distracted by anything else while you're in the room. To be the thing he's thinking about, even when you're not there. She looks up to see Wil join the table, his gaze hovering as if reading her thoughts.

'Jesus you two,' Mel says, rolling her eyes at Cooper. 'The Marriot called, they've got a room. Now, can we bring the focus back to the fact that the woman over there is freakin' kickass?'

'Who?' Tyler asks as he joins them, dragging over a stool and opening a can of Red Bull.

'Her, with brown hair next to Thommo. That's Stacey Gorman, she runs the tour.' Mel loves collecting stories of women making their mark in the world. She shares them with whoever will listen – or whoever she makes listen.

'What,' Tyler says, 'even the guys'?'

'Oh right, here we go,' Mel snaps. Who invited the boys to the table anyway? The mood always changes when they're around. Or maybe it's just her mood that changes. Either way, it's *on*.

'It's a fair enough question, though,' Wil adds calmly, while Cooper buries his head into Jaspa's hair, keen to get out of the firing line.

'Is it? Is it, William?' Mel stands up, places her back-pack on the stool and unzips it. 'So, if it was a dude running the whole tour, including the women's, you'd ask the same thing?' Her mouth tightens and she stares from Wil to Tyler, who both struggle to find an answer.

'She's right, you wouldn't,' Cooper says through strands of Jaspa's hair.

'No.' Mel stuffs her towel and jacket into the back-pack and swings it onto her shoulder. 'You would not. Shall we go?' She looks from Carolyn to Jaspa.

'Oh, um, sure.' Jaspa slowly gets up and takes Cooper's hand. 'Should we all walk home together?'

Mel pauses, then lets out a frustrated sigh. 'Yeah, sure, whatever.' She bolts ahead and stops where Thomas is sitting. 'Hi,' she says, offering her hand to Stacey. 'I just wanted to say I think it's amazing to have a female running the show.'

Thomas puts down his coffee, wipes a napkin over his mouth and swallows. 'Stacey, this is Melissa Appleby.'

'Mel is fine,' Mel says, then smirks. 'Unless I do something bad that warrants you hollering my whole name.'

'*Mel*,' Thomas accentuates, 'is a student at the Insti-tute of Sporting Excellence, one of our star juniors.'

Stacey smiles and takes off her sunglasses. Mel

notices her eyes; the creases celebrate each laugh she's had in life. So much more beautiful than the botoxed abominations she sees struggling for expression around the upper waterway suburbs of Pacific Grove. When Mel's mum said she was considering botox – no doubt after a backhanded comment from her dad – Mel replied, *no frickin' way*. Not only does it look ridiculous, it costs the same as a flight to Bali. Priorities, please!

'It's a pleasure to meet you, Mel. I actually already know a bit about you,' Stacey says.

'You do?' Mel's stomach flips. What the heck has Thommo told her? Surely not about the time she skipped school and hitchhiked to the Bryon Bay Surf Fest?

'Yes, I do. I read the letter you and your friends posted. The Bikini Collective?'

'Oh! Yes, that's right, The Bikini Collective.' Mel can't wait to tell Jaspa and Carolyn that even the head of the tour saw the letter they wrote to *Salt Action*.

'Oh sorry, please excuse me, it was lovely to meet you.' Stacey picks up the phone buzzing on the table and flips open the wave-patterned case. 'Stacey speaking.'

'Nice to meet you,' Mel mouths in a whisper, then spots Carolyn at the stairs waving her over. 'I've gotta go, see you later Mr Sampson.'

'Okay, Mel, see you all back home. Don't get into any trouble between here and there.' He picks up his coffee and points it towards her before taking a sip. 'I'm trusting you all to do the right thing.'

Trouble? What kind of trouble could she get into between here and the house? It's only 700 metres away. *Sheesh.*

#7

'Three, four, five ... oh.' Jaspa, Cooper, Tyler and Carolyn count as they surround Mel and Wil to see who can hold the longest handstand. Wil topples over backwards while Mel drives her hands further into the sand.

'Bro, you let her *smash* you,' Tyler says through cupped hands while Wil lies on his back, defeated.

Mel screws up her face as her arms begin to shake. A loud grunt escapes her lips as she unlocks her elbows and lands on her feet. 'How do those words taste, William? Nice and bitter?' she says through short breaths.

'Next time, Appleby.' Wil stands up and brushes down his pants, then walks over to Mel, holding out his hand. As she goes to shake it he whips it away and smooths it over his hair, attempting to hold back a smirk.

'Oh, like that is it?' Mel says, looking up at him and putting her hand on her cocked hip. 'Don't worry, William. I'm sure losing becomes easier over time, although I wouldn't know,' Mel says over shoulder as she swivels to pick up her surfboard and backpack. She struggles to feed one of her arms through the strap, which is twisted and stuck on a buckle.

'Here, let me help you with that,' Wil offers, reaching out his hand.

'No thank you,' Mel says, wincing away. 'I'm fine.' Her arm contorts to try and unravel the mess behind her until she gets so flustered that she drops her surfboard on the sand, pulls the backpack off and fixes the twisted strap.

'You know it's not a sign of weakness to accept someone's offer of help?' Wil says with raised eyebrows, stifling a giggle.

'You know it's called stalking when you hover close to someone uninvited?' Mel, now fully assembled, picks up her board and jogs to catch up to Jaspa and Carolyn.

'Urgh, he's so annoying,' she says.

'Yeah right,' Carolyn draws out, giving Jaspa a sideways glance.

'What? What the heck was that look for?' Mel is

okay with dishing out the jokes, but not being the brunt of them.

'We just think …' Jaspa stops.

'What? You just think what?'

'We just think that you and Wil are into each other.' Jaspa spits out the last part of the sentence, then leans on Carolyn's shoulder, giggling.

'Yuck. You two are truly delusional – I think you should be medically examined.' There's no freakin' way Mel wants to hook up with William Sanders. Sure, he's cute, but he's just so blah. Why would she waste scoring potential on a guy from Pacific Grove when the world is her oyster for boys – her *boyster*. She has to choose wisely and find someone who has a level of importance. Someone everybody else wants. She'll find the hottest and most charismatic boy in the room and make herself irresistible to him with her playful banter and a cocked eyebrow. Not that she's an expert on boyfriends. Pash and dashes, well that's another thing entirely.

'Well, you could do way worse,' Carolyn says as they reach the steps leading up to the house.

Mel heaves herself up behind Jaspa, whose long legs make an effortless ascent. 'I don't want to do even slightly worse. I want to do way extraordinary. Hey, what's that?' Music starts to blare from 50 metres up the beach. 'C'mon, let's suss it out.' As they walk past their house, along the skinny concrete walkway, the sound of laughter, splashing and clinking glasses grows louder. The path ends, blocked by a three metre-high glass wall.

Inside they see a guy in baggy hot-pink floral boardshorts drinking from a champagne bottle before taking off his shirt in a pretend striptease and launching himself into the pool, splashing three girls who are lying on sun lounges. 'What can I say, you hot bitches needed cooling off,' the guy says when they protest. 'There's only so much divine eye candy a poor boy like me can handle. Now, gimme gimme, fill that glass.' He wiggles his hand. 'I'm getting withdrawals already.'

Mel turns to Jaspa and Carolyn. 'Let's go in, he looks fun!'

'We can't.' Jaspa points to a sign. 'It's a private beach club.'

Mel leans against the glass and cups her hands around her eyes. 'There must be a way.'

The guy swims to the end of the pool towards the girls, holding his glass above the water, taking sips as he goes. 'You,' he shouts dramatically. 'You, goddess, come in here immediately.'

Mel peels her face from the glass and turns to face Jaspa.

'I'm talking about you, Pineapple. Get that tush of

yours in here pronto before my heart disintegrates into a billion sad face emojis.'

A blankness swipes over Mel's face before she looks at the pineapple print on her backpack and laughs. 'But it says private property,' she calls through the glass.

'Don't fear, my pretties.' He props himself up on the side of the pool, adjusting his shorts where his brown tummy flops over the top. 'That's just Papa's way of keeping commoners out. But not goddesses. Go down the side to the second gate and Vincent will let you in. And bring your friends. Vincent,' he yells. 'Three gifts from the heavens incoming.'

Mel picks up her board. 'C'mon, let's go.'

Jaspa looks back towards their house. 'We're supposed to be heading straight home. I'd better tell Cooper.'

'Are you freakin' serious, Jazz?' Mel releases a groan. 'You're not actually welded to his mind. You do have one of your own, you know. Carolyn?'

'Not me, dude. I'm bailing home to eat and nap out.'

'Jesus, seriously guys?' Mel turns and tugs on Jaspa's arm. 'Jaspa, please do this for me, just for halfa? We're in LA, and we're being invited into an exclusive club,' she whispers through clenched teeth. 'C'mon, c'mon, c'mon, c'm–'

Jaspa releases a sigh. 'Okay. Just thirty minutes though, so Mr Sampson doesn't get mad.'

'Yes! See you soon, Carolyn. Cover for us.' Mel embraces Jaspa then pulls her by the arm until they reach a door, which is opened by a tall man dressed in black and wearing earbud headphones.

'Ladies, this way please,' he says, ushering them down a garden path towards the pool.

Floral shorts guy stands up and gasps dramatically, covering his face with his hands. 'Oh shut the front door, you're surfer girls?'

> *'We're wave trimmin'*
> *but everything's not fine*
> *Cos we're wave trimming*
> *but you won't be miiiiiiine.'*

He sings while raising his hands and wiggling his hips.

'Ooh, you like Double Denim too?' Mel squeals, placing her surfboard on the grass.

'Oh yes.' He picks up a towel and starts patting it over his arms, which are covered in goosebumps. 'The lead singer, Lauren, is a Salvie.'

'A whatie?' Mel asks, wondering if that's an American version of Salvo, like Salvation Army.

'A Salvie. I'm Salvador Perez Junior,' He rolls his hand in the air with a flourish and bows to them. 'And my carefully selected friends of the female kind are called Salvies,' he giggles. 'Which I now officially declare you to be, because you're outstanding, and do I detect an accent from down under? Let's all just marry now and call each other cobber. Kangaroos can be our flower girls, yes?' Mel looks at Jaspa and they laugh at his attempt to mimic an Australian.

'Yeah, we're both from Bonita Shores, it's on the north coast. Well, the north of the east coast. I'm Mel, this is Jaspa,' Mel says, reaching out to shake Salvador's hand.

'Handshake? I think not.' He opens his arms and waves his hands. 'Come, come.' Mel coaxes Jaspa in and they form a group hug. 'It's my ultimate of pleasures to meet you, Jaspa. And you might be Mel to the world, but to me you will always be Pineapple. Now, can I get you a drink?' Salvador picks up the bottle of champagne and wiggles it.

'Oh, no thanks,' Jaspa blurts.

'Not right now,' Mel counters, as though getting asked to drink French champagne at three in the afternoon is an actual thing. Mel teeters between thinking alcohol is for losers when she's in surf comp mode, and having a sneaky few on the rare occasion that she's swept away in the moment. But for the most part, she'd rather leave drinking and weed to those who aren't gunning to win a world surfing title. Plus, the one hangover she copped after too much punch, which tasted fruity and delicious but most definitely had lashings of vodka, at Serena Smith's eighteenth birthday was enough to convince her to party sober. She'd woken at 10 am with chunks of chuck dried to her face and throughout her hair, and a headache pounding so violently against her skull that she was convinced she'd had an aneurysm. And that wasn't even the worst part. Paradise Point was five foot perfection that day, but she couldn't peel herself out of bed. 'We're actually surfing in a comp.'

'And you're here for how long?' Salvador asks, pulling three beanbags onto the deck.

'A bit over a week,' Mel says. She notices Jaspa hesitating to sit down, so subtly mouths *just another fifteen minutes*.

'A week, ooh goodie,' he claps. 'Plenty of time for me to corrupt you.'

#8

'Yes, go Jazz, go!' Mel leaps up to hoot through cupped hands, sending her stool toppling over behind her. 'Oops, sorry about that,' she says to the two girls it almost hit. 'That's my bestie out there ripping it up.' The girls smile weakly and continue swiping through Instagram. Mel hops back onto her stool and takes a sip of her hot chocolate. The competitors' area is starting to fill up, and the smell of stir-fry being served for lunch is torturing her nostrils. She had a croissant and a bowl of fruit for breakfast, but that was almost five hours ago. Her stomach grumbles in protest. 'Just wait until after my heat, lil buddy,' she says, patting it.

'Yakking to yourself again, weirdo?' Carolyn dead-pans as she approaches the table, drying her hair with a towel.

'Oh hey, *chica*. Man, I'm so sorry you didn't get through.' Mel pulls out a stool for Carolyn. 'It was really tough, looked like the ocean just turned off the wave tap every time you were in position.'

'Yeah, well, just my luck. I also blew it falling on my best wave.'

'I saw that, what the heck happened?'

'Just the ol' wax slip splits.'

'It didn't help that you drew Gloria Cruz. That chick is so good it's ridiculous.'

Carolyn rests her head down in her hands and shakes it. 'Argh, I'm so pissed.'

'Hey, don't smash yourself up about it.' Mel reaches over and cups Carolyn's shoulder. 'Onwards, upwards and dominate, okay? Plus at least now you get to sleep in.'

'Yep. And I'm gonna pig myself stupid on that buffet.' She gets up.

'Atta girl!' Mel says. She wishes she was as good at comforting herself through losses. She prides herself on learning from them, but not before the steam rises and disappointment weighs her down.

She's made plenty of finals, but she's only won one contest. It was at Sydney's North Narrabeen beach last March, in the final against local Jess Steel, who led in first place. With only one minute remaining in the heat,

Mel needed an 8.1 to win. Jess had earned priority to take whatever wave she wanted next, so she kept close to Mel to prevent her from winning. No matter which direction Mel paddled, Jess followed, so closely that their boards were practically touching. Mel's breath was short and her head hung low against her surfboard, allowing the water to lap against her hair. Then she heard someone whistle from the beach. She looked up to see an overhead-high set approaching. Her watch blinked: 40 seconds remaining.

Mel scratched through the water into position, but Jess cut her off and used her priority to take the ride. From the back of the wave Mel could see Jess attempt a top turn, but heard a thud as she fell against the water. In a flash, Mel swung around to catch the second wave in the set, which was half a foot bigger than the first. Her feet reached the board before the siren sounded, meaning the wave would be scored. This was her final chance. She was quick to her feet and the wall of water stood up tall in front of her. Drawing out a deep back-hand bottom turn, she angled the nose of her board vertical into the crest of the wave and thrust on her back foot to release her fins. She leaned on her front foot to pump through the next section and tucked into a cover of water, holding the rail of her board to keep tight in the barrel, tunnelling towards the light. She was catapulted to meet the closeout section, right where Jess and the other finalists were paddling in to shore. Lining herself up with the pitch of the wave, Mel cracked her board into the pocket, finishing the turn right on the sand, where she hopped off her board in a running motion and held her arms high in victory.

'How's Jaspa doin'?' Carolyn returns to the table with her plate piled higher than the Malibu hills to find Mel deep in thought. 'Hello, anyone home? Is Jaspa gonna get through?'

'Oh, hey.' Mel sits upright and steals a piece of carrot from Carolyn's lunch and pops it in her mouth. 'Yeah, she's ruling. Her style's so smooth, it makes me sick!' Mel smirks. 'Oh, go, GO!' She drums her hands on the table as Jaspa paddles for another playful wave that glides into the point.

Mel has been competing against Jaspa in the Bonita Shores Boardriders' rounds since they were ten, back when they were the only two girls. Thinking back, it's obvious the judging (by dads, brothers, etc.) was a little rigged, because first and second place would alternate from month to month. The club now has five female members under 18, and more showing interest since the girls started The Bikini Collective. One day they hope to branch off and run their own girls-only club.

'Hey chicks.' Cooper slides onto a stool with Tyler

and Wil standing close behind him. 'Looks like Jazz just got through.' How can one word variation irk Mel so much? Jaspa's family members call her Jazz on occasion, so why does it bother her when Cooper does it? Because he's *not* family. Mel might not be either, at least not by blood, but they're as tight as sisters.

'Alrighty.' Mel springs up. 'I'm the heat after next, so wish me a win.'

'Good luck,' Wil offers through a timid, somewhat dreamy, smile.

'I said a win.'

'Oh,' he stumbles. 'Good win.'

Mel turns her back with a cheeky grin and heads to the competitors' board rack. She picks up her five-four swallowtail, which she's hoping will soar nicely over today's slightly sluggish waves. She contorts her body into her wetsuit and carries her board downstairs to collect her blue competition vest. As she walks up to the paddle-out spot she hears a 'Hey!' from behind.

Jaspa is coming in from her heat with Thomas debriefing next to her. 'Yew!' Mel calls back. 'That was awesome, Jazz!' See, when *she* says it, it feels just perfect. 'Any tips?'

'Oh, I dunno, just catch waves I guess.' Asking Jaspa about competition tactics is futile; she barely has a clue how scores are determined or how smart strategy can change the course of a heat. 'Good luck!' she adds.

'Good luck, Mel,' Thomas repeats. 'Get your first two rides quickly and then you can concentrate on waiting for a bigger set. The ocean's a little slow with the incoming tide.'

'Thanks, Mr Sampson. I think you mean good win!' Mel laughs at him shaking his head, then continues towards the rocks and paddles out.

Right from the sound of the siren marking the start of her heat, Mel shows no mercy for her competitors. She returns from her second ride and powers straight past them to sit deep and wait for a bigger wave.

Her legs swirl underneath the board and she turns to face the shore. Five hundred metres north is the beach club. It sits on the edge of the cliff, overhanging the ocean like a massive dollop of white cream. With its smooth walls and dramatic arches, the building would look more at home on a Spanish ranch than here, so close to the Los Angeles bustle. Mel's mind wanders to when she was there yesterday afternoon. She chuckled at the memory of Salvador asking Tiffany to make him up. *He looks better in red lippy than I do*, Mel thinks, letting out an audible laugh. Turns out Tiffany's the daughter of Pamela Bates, the actress from the space zombie movie *Mars Rising* that Mel and Jaspa saw last year. Jaspa had nightmares for days afterwards.

The commentator jolts Mel from her thoughts. 'Angela Jones in yellow, you're in fourth place, requiring a combination score of 12.3 to progress into second. Surfer in blue, Melissa Appleby, you're in third on 11.5 and require a 6.8 for second place to progress on to round three. Surfers, there are four minutes remaining.'

Whoa. Mel's heart thumps against her ribcage. How did her competitors push her out of position? They must've caught some inside waves she didn't see. She stares determinedly at the ocean and takes over-exaggerated breaths in and out through her nose. She has priority to choose which wave she catches, so she tries to summon some patience, which comes about as naturally to her as subtlety. The digits on her watch tell here there are just over two minutes remaining. She'll have to take the set that's approaching. A perfectly-formed line of swell glides towards her, its surface like a sheet of glass, ready to be broken apart.

What should she do? Usually she would choose the second wave in the set, as it would be better formed and deliver more power. But what if there is no second wave? Mel leaves the first and paddles over the top of it. Mel Appleby doesn't settle for mediocre. It's a risk, but she's confident there'll be something bigger and better on the horizon. Her competitors are thrown off guard; they expected her to take that ride, so didn't paddle for it themselves. They curse under their breath. That move could change the positions of the entire heat.

The commentator ramps up the suspense. 'Surfer in blue, there are 30 seconds remaining. I repeat, 30 seconds remaining.'

Mel paddles so strongly over the first wave that she's sent airborne onto the other side. And there it is. The second wave standing up in front of her, daring her to take it. In a swift move, she whips her board around to face the shore, takes two strong strokes, pushing her hands through the water and keeping them close to her board to increase her pace, then jumps to her feet with the pitching lip. This wave is anything but sluggish, its direction creating a perfect form along the sandbank.

After the take-off, Mel steers her board to reach the base of the wave and leans her body towards the water so she pivots onto the rail of fibreglass. Speed carries her from bottom to top, and as her board reaches the curl of ocean it projects her into a dynamic turn, sending spray twice her height into the air. Everything feels right. She immediately transitions into another top turn, then grabs the rail with her right hand to swoop into a cutback from the open stretch of blue back into the pocket of foam. The wave halves in size and trickles into shore and Mel rides in, standing tall with her arms above her in a prayer sign. She didn't just make it to the next round, she won the heat, and posted the highest wave score of the day.

Mel loves it here. She's winning and she's surrounded by exciting people doing exciting things. At last, Mel *belongs* somewhere.

#9

Mel studies herself in the mirror. Lucky she packed a dress and heels. She pinches the material either side of her hips and shuffles it around so the side split sits comfortably on her left thigh. The strapless padded bra at least allows her a bit of boob to fill out the gaping neckline, but it feels uncomfortable as hell.

'Jesus, I honestly don't know how you wear these harnesses every day of your life,' she says to Jaspa, who's riffling through her suitcase for ankle boots.

'Wow, you look stunning,' Jaspa says, looking up. 'Is that the dress you wore to the boardriders banquet last year?'

'Yeah, see?' Mel points to a faint mark just under the right strap. 'Remnants of the food fight. Guacamole, from memory.'

'Sure as hell was,' Carolyn says, coming out of the bathroom dressed in a boobtube pants suit. 'I got you real good.'

Mel sees Carolyn appear in the reflection behind her and swings around. 'Look at you! You're not in jeans and a T-shirt!' Mel pushes Carolyn onto the bed and opens her make-up bag. 'Now sit down, this won't hurt a bit.'

'Not too much or I'm washing it all off.'

'Don't worry, you can trust me.' Mel pulls a mascara brush out of the tube. 'It's not like I owe you guacamole payback or anything, mwa-ha-ha!'

Carolyn screws up her face as Mel holds her chin and strokes the brush upwards onto her lashes. 'There,' Mel says, putting the mascara back into her bag. 'Look at those baby browns.'

'Girls!' Thomas bellows from downstairs, then draws in a long breath. 'Be down in five please, the driver is waiting.'

Mel picks up her black mesh clutch bag and pops a tube of pawpaw ointment inside, then holds open the bedroom door and waves Jaspa and Carolyn through. 'Ready for the red carpet?' The three girls giggle and head downstairs to the stretch Hummer that's waiting in the driveway.

Mel can't quite believe the Australian surf team has

been invited to the premiere of *Wave Race*. It's a new animated movie, and the trailer looks hilarious. All they know is it's about a new zoo in the Californian desert where all the animals are segregated according to their countries of origin and refuse to mix with each other. It gets nasty and racist until a Mexican spider monkey decides it's had enough and organises a secret monthly midnight surfing club in the zoo's wave pool. Famous actors and actresses did the voices, and the theme song, 'Ride With Me', has reached number one in thirteen countries before the movie has even been released.

Mel squeals as they drive along Hollywood Boulevard and pull up outside Grauman's Chinese Theatre. 'Look!' she says, leaning her entire body over Jaspa and Cooper to peer through the tinted window. 'Is that freakin' Ed Sheeran? And there, over there,' she taps on the glass. 'That dude's got a TMZ mic! There are cameras everywhere! This is off the hook!'

A partition glides back and Thomas turns around from the front seat. 'Okay you lot, as you can see, we're here. I expect you to act like responsible adults.'

'Well, we're not technically adults yet, Mr Sampson,' Mel interrupts while shuffling herself towards the door. 'We're only fifteen, so cannot be restricted to adult behaviours.'

He lets out a light-hearted sigh. 'You know very

well what I mean, Melissa. I'll be keeping an eye on you especially. Now get out there and enjoy yourselves, but remember, we all stick together. Understood?'

The entire back of the Hummer erupts with a chorus of 'Yes, Mr Sampson,' followed by a succession of excited laughs. A man in a white tuxedo opens the door, and as Mel's heel hits the red carpet her tummy flips in anticipation. 'Ladies.' She threads Carolyn's arm through her bent elbow, then pulls Jaspa's hand out of Cooper's and links her on the other side. 'Let's take a red carpet ride, shall we?'

Rows of screaming fans lean over the barricade, waving their phones and begging their favourite stars for a selfie. Paparazzi cameras flash from all directions and celebrities are ushered aside for interviews. A Flowrider wave machine has been set up in the street and is being surfed by someone in a monkey suit. They're actually pretty good. Mel wonders if it's someone from the contest.

'Girls, girls, come over here.'

Mel, Jaspa and Carolyn swing around to see Trudy Hardwick calling them over. They greet her at a backdrop decorated with the movie's title and sponsors' logos. 'I feel like such a dork standing here posing alone, help me out!' She lines the girls up around her. 'Now, smile.' Cameras click and people with notepads keep shouting, 'What are your names, who are you?'

'Put "The Bikini Collective",' Trudy responds. 'And follow my Instagram to see what we have planned next week.' As she's whisked away for another interview, Trudy calls back over her shoulder, 'I'll chat to you later about our surf day. Have fun tonight.'

Mel turns to the others, wide-eyed. 'I'm so excited I can't promise I won't piss myself.' Mel and Carolyn laugh when Jaspa takes it literally and suggests they should perhaps go to the toilet then. They wait at the main entrance with Thomas and the other surfers who're staying in their Malibu house. 'There they are,' Mel says, pointing to the rest of the Australian surf team, who are walking towards them, the manager Greg Warren and his assistants following close behind.

If someone had told Mel a year ago that she'd be surfing in a world junior event, staying at a beachfront Malibu mansion, invited to walk the red carpet of Hollywood's hottest film, and launching a Bikini Collective event with Trudy Hardwick, she would've told them to get the heck outta here. Nothing like this would ever happen in boring Bonita Shores.

She glances at Cooper. He's rubbing his hand along Jaspa's lower back as they talk and laugh with the other surfers. His eyes switch onto high beam every time he looks at her. She says something innocently funny and he pulls her in tight. Mel drops her gaze. That's the only thing missing from this perfect moment – she hasn't got a date. She's here with her best friend, but her best friend wants to be with her boyfriend. Mel's caught Wil giving her several lingering looks from afar, but he's not who she wants. She wants better.

'Pineapple!' A yell from the crowd jolts her out of her thoughts. She hears it again. 'Pineapple!' She sees Salvador waving frantically and pushing his way through the crowd gathered on the red carpet.

She cups her hands over her mouth and stomps her feet excitedly on the spot. Salvador rushes towards her with his arms outstretched, wearing a maroon suit covered in a pattern of cherry blossoms.

'Salvador!' Mel says as he smothers her in an exaggerated embrace. 'What are you doing here? Your suit is amazing.'

'Darling,' he says with a flick of his hand. 'Papa practically *made* this movie. Who do you think the ever-charismatic Seb the Mexican spider monkey is based on, mmm?' Salvador dances around with one hand scratching his head and the other under his armpit.

'You're still not telling everyone you're the monkey, are you?' a voice says playfully from behind him.

'Oh, you little bitch, come here immediately.' He

swoops an arm around the girl's waist. 'Mel, you remember Susie, *si?*'

Mel grins and nods. 'Awesome to see you again, I love your hat.' She tries to avoid looking at Susie's chest, where her breasts threaten to leap out of her dress at any moment. And the orange tinge to her skin must be fake, surely? Susie Rey rose to instant fame after appearing on reality television show *Boarding School Babes*, and soon became an online favourite because she built a flying fox-like escape route from her dorm window to sneak out each night. The memes went nuts, showing Susie flying-foxing into all kinds of scenes, like the mouth of a shark or an Ariana Grande concert. Mel's favourite was one that had her going from the Sydney Harbour Bridge down to the Opera House while avoiding snapping crocodiles. All of them had her catchphrase in thick, bold font: 'THAT'S TAPPED!'

'Hey, we're heading into our seats now, you coming?'

Mel looks around to see Jaspa beside her, still holding onto Cooper's hand while he talks to Wil and Tyler. 'Oh, yeah I was just–'

'Jaspa!' Salvador cuts in with a squeal. 'You're just like a mythical mermaid.' His eyes widen and he sucks in his cheeks. 'Who is that Adonis your body is connected to and why have you kept him from me all this time? I thought we were friends!'

Jaspa giggles and pulls Cooper towards them. 'Babe, this is Salvador, the guy we were telling you about.'

Salvador gasps. 'You were talking about *me*, to *him*?' He places a hand on his chest, feigning disbelief. 'Who's got powder, I need powder, I'm all shiny with excitement.' Susie opens her compact and dabs the sponge over Salvador's nose and forehead while laughter erupts around them.

Cooper holds his free hand out to Salvador. 'Nice to meet you, man. I hear you showed the girls a good time at that beach club.'

'Oh handsome, they ain't seen nothin' yet.' He links arms with Mel and pulls her in close. 'Is it champagne o'clock yet?' He looks around for the waiters carrying trays of drinks.

'How do you even get served? Don't you have to be twenty-one in America?' Mel asks.

'Oh, Pineapple, it's not about *being* twenty-one, it's about *believing* you're twenty-one, right Susie?' Salvador takes the glass Susie offers him and they clink with a giggle.

Mel hears a mumble behind her. 'Dudes, let's go, this guy's totally gay.' Her eyes burn into Tyler and she hopes no one else heard his remark. She catches Mr

Sampson waving them over, so pats Salvador's arm. 'Hey, we have to go, that's our teacher and he's already dirty on us for sneaking off to your club the other day.' She leans over to kiss Susie on the cheek, keen to avoid suffocation by boob embrace, then draws Salvador in for a big hug and gives him her number. 'Let's catch up, we're here for another six days.'

As she walks away with the others, her phone beeps with a message from Salvador. It's a screen full of pineapple and heart emojis. She turns around to wave her phone at him, then freezes in disbelief. It's the guy from the beach. It's definitely him – he has the same palm tree tattoo on his arm. And he's talking to Salvador.

#10

The glow from Mel's phone lights up her doona cocoon. She can hear Jaspa's breathing, deep and rhythmic, and Carolyn's nose has been gurgling for the past twenty minutes. She pushes her phone further under the doona to avoid waking them. Her finger is aching but she continues to scroll, searching for photos. Well, one photo in particular.

Mel believes in love at first sight. That tidal wave of nerves swirling in your stomach when you see that certain someone. The room spins around you, like you're standing still in the moment but the world keeps going. When they smile at you it's like sweet, warm melted butter is being poured over your heart. You feel like every movement you make with them, linking hands, a lean on a shoulder, a synchronised giggle, is as much a perfect fit as riding a wave – the grace you feel when you time every turn perfectly, or when the ocean rewards you with a set when it's only you waiting.

Mel's only had that feeling twice before. Once with Kazumi Hall, the teenage world champion surfer she met at the final qualifying event last year. He invited her to a party and wouldn't leave her side. He whispered into her ear how beautiful she looked and he introduced her to all his friends. He cupped her cheek and draped his fingers over the back of her neck, stroking it softly. He pulled her onto his lap when there were no other spare seats, and wrapped his arms tight around her waist. He used a skateboard to show her how to get more airs into her turns. It's all about sliding the front foot up, he said. When their mouths met he would pepper small pecks around her lips before drawing her in for a deeper kiss. His body leaned into her, and when his tongue brushed against hers, prickles erupted all over her body.

But it all fell away the moment she saw him walking off with another girl. Mel had only been in the bathroom for two minutes and there he was, cupping the waist of someone else. First her cheeks reddened. It was embarrassing. Then the emotion filled her eyes. She really liked him, he was exactly the kind of guy she wanted to be with. Someone who was *known* for something.

The second time was two days ago at the beach, and then tonight at the movie premiere. The same guy.

And, bingo! She clicks on the photo and enlarges it. There he is, smiling on the red carpet with Salvador and Susie. The caption says he is Corey Swain. And Google reveals that he's listed as one of California's top ten artists to watch.

#11

Mel leans out the window of the passenger seat, still trying to get used to it being on the other side of the car. 'Jazz, Jesus, c'mon, we'll only be a few hours. You can suck face later.' She shuffles her fingers through her hair, squeezing the excess water onto the pavement. Despite being awake half the night, she went out for a sunrise surf with Jaspa, leaving Carolyn to sleep in. The waves were gliding in from the north like a perfectly aligned flock of birds. The surface was like a covering of polished crystal, and each manoeuvre they performed flowed from one transition to the next, with no resistance.

'Chop chop, lover!' Mel calls.

Jaspa parts lips with Cooper and waves towards the car parked in the driveway. 'Sorry, guys. I just wanted to wish him luck,' she says, easing into the back seat next to Carolyn. 'He's in heat three.' The boys' competition is on today, which means the girls have a lay-day. 'I feel a bit bad not watching him, he always supports me.'

Mel turns from the front seat and grins. 'I know, but then who will support me and all the shopping bags I have to carry?'

'Are we all strapped in?' asks Grace, the assistant surf team manager. She steers the car around the wide circular driveway and veers south onto the Pacific Coast Highway. A morning mist shades the sun from full exposure, and it seems there's not even enough wind to blow a grain of sand. The surface of the sea is as smooth as a backyard swimming pool, only broken up by lines of waves marching in from the horizon.

Mel gasps. 'Ooh, it's coming up!' She zooms in on the GPS screen. 'Are we turning up Santa Monica Boulevard? Please, please, please?'

Grace laughs. 'Of course. It's not a trip to LA if you haven't been to Santa Monica. I thought we could grab a juice or something here, then head to the pier.'

Mel glances back at Jaspa and Carolyn and jiggles her arms in the air in a little dance. The car pulls onto Santa Monica Boulevard for just 200 metres before turning down a side street and pulling into a car park. They pile out of the car and walk towards the beachfront before Grace stops outside a coffee shop called Espress to Impress.

'This is one of my favourite places,' Grace says excitedly. 'The deal is, you order a coffee or chai or whatever and get a flavoured whipped cream on top. There's cinnamon, mint, chocolate … so many, take your pick. I'll have the nutty nutmeg please,' she says over the counter before turning around. 'You brought your keep cups, yeah?'

The girls nod and Mel groans in delight. 'Seriously, it smells so delicious in here my nostrils will never forgive me for leaving. What flavour are you having?' she asks Jaspa.

'Umm …' Jaspa looks down at the menu in her hand. 'I can't decide between vanilla with rose petal or —'

'Dude.' Carolyn cuts in, scrunching up her face. 'Flowers do *not* belong in whipped cream.'

'She's right, Jazz. Go for something way more sinister. Let me order for you.' Mel collects the girls' cups, goes to the counter and places them in front of the waitress with a grin. 'Hi, how are ya? Okay, I'll have mine with chilli cacao, Jaspa will have almond fudge and, what did you decide, Carolyn?'

'Rocky road.'

'Oh hell yeah, good choice. She'll have rocky road

please.' Mel turns around to Grace. 'You're a legend, thanks for showing us around. Where are the other chicks today?'

Grace picks up her order and licks the cream from the side of the cup. 'Oh, they decided to stay home and study, which you will also have to do at some point.'

Mel sneers. She's just getting used to the concept of a nice long vacation, she's not ready to be jolted back to reality just yet.

They walk to the front of the Santa Monica pier and take a selfie, then hop on the ferris wheel. It travels to the top and hovers there.

'You know, I don't know why this beach is so famous,' Jaspa says awkwardly. She's never comfortable raising controversial opinions. 'It's quite ugly. Bonita is so much more beautiful.'

'But you would never be bored here,' Mel says, wiping her finger around the inside rim of her cup and licking it while looking at the view below. There are people *everywhere*. They've travelled from all over the world to visit this exact spot. 'There are endless possibilities for excitement here.' She thinks back to the photo of Corey she took a screenshot of last night and keeps gawking at every ten minutes. She wants to ask Salvador to introduce them, but feels uncharacteristically nervous. Then again, she's pretty sure he'll do anything for her. She makes a mental note to message him for intel as they hop off the ferris wheel and head south along the ocean front.

'Oh my god, this is insane, where are we?' Mel asks Grace. They've walked along a palm-fringed promenade and have reached a group of hip-hop dancers who are performing in the street with music blaring. They're wearing matching red glitter Adidas tracksuits and are nailing backflips and jumping into the splits. Just down from them is a man with two gigantic pythons wrapped around his body, and next to him, a contortionist places her feet over her shoulders and begins walking around on her hands.

'This,' Grace says, pushing the girls aside as a group of rollerskaters almost bowl them over, 'is the famous Venice Beach.'

Mel turns on the spot and takes it all in. The sky is completely cloudless and the sun offers enough warmth that she only needs a light jacket. Artists exhibit their work along the pavement, beckoning people in for a sale. Four older Rastafarians, with dark dreadlocks down to the waist and wearing striped beanies, sit at a small table playing cards, laughing with such guttural joy that Mel wonders what's so funny.

She sees a couple of surfers walk by, still wet from the ocean. Past the sand, poorly formed closeout waves pound onto the shore. Mel releases a silent sigh of relief – no risk of surf FOMO here. They stop to watch the action in the huge skate park that's almost on the sand. A girl lends Carolyn her board and Mel films her weaving up and down the walls, carving and high-fiving people as she goes. She drops into the steepest section and pops an air on the other side, right in front of two little girls. Mel hears them tell their mother they want to learn skating too. The boy next to them protests that they can't because they're girls. They tell him that's ridiculous.

When Carolyn finally returns the borrowed board, they walk from the beach back to the main thorough-fare. The further south they go, the more residential it becomes. They turn left down a narrow alleyway and it's as if they've entered a different world. Houses line a series of canals with quaint wooden bridges spanning the water.

'Holy crap.' Mel pulls out her phone and snaps a series of pictures. 'This is just like a movie set.' Perfectly clipped hedges line the front of the homes, and palm trees are dotted along the canal. Boats and canoes are tied to the railings. Mel imagines how cool it would be if they lived here – they could row to each other's houses and have little boat parties. As the others walk ahead, Mel stops at a front yard and stares intently. It's not like the other homes around it, which are flash and manicured. This house is single storey and planked with blue sheets of weathered fibro. Vines creep around the exterior. The gate's open, so Mel sneaks into the yard for a closer look. The garden is overgrown and a selection of paints and half-decorated pottery is scattered on the veranda. But what catches Mel's eye is the collection of surfboards at the side of the house. There must be about thirty, of all different shapes and sizes, piled up on top of one another.

'See a ride you like, dear?' croaks a voice from the bushes.

'Jesus!' Mel jumps and her heart smacks against her chest. 'I, I umm ...' She steadies herself on the picket fence as the lady comes into full view, clutching a handful of weeds and a trowel. Her grey hair is pulled into a waist-length ponytail and her leathered skin is etched with lines. She yanks up her floral cotton flares with one hand so she can step over a shrub to reach Mel.

'You kinda scared me,' Mel says.

'I tend to have that effect on people.' The woman cackles and reveals several gaps where her teeth used to be.

Mel shifts her weight onto her back foot and glances down the embankment to see the others walking slowly.

She should catch up to them, this place is giving her the creeps. 'I, err, I should be going. Sorry I trespassed.'

'I think you'll be more sorry if you don't stay.'

'Pardon?'

'Well, something drew you here. Why don't you step inside and discover what that is?'

Mel tilts her head back. She should tell the others where she is, but she is curious. Surely she's not going to be murdered in broad daylight? She tightens her grip on her keep cup, wondering if she can use it as a makeshift weapon. 'Well, okay, sure. But my friends are just there.' *And just so you know, I can scream really frickin' loud.* She follows the woman over to the veranda.

'What's your name?' Mel asks.

'It's Claudia, dear.'

'Oh, hi, my name's M–'

'No, no, don't tell me.' She holds up a bony hand and presses a crooked finger to her lips. 'All will reveal itself in time.'

What the heck's that supposed to mean? Mel wonders. She should bolt, but it's too late, she's already on the veranda. And curiosity is trumping sensibility.

Claudia gestures to a beanbag, encouraging Mel to plonk down, then kneels beside her on a silk purple cushion. 'May I have your hand, dear?'

Mel's brow furrows. 'My what? Why?'

'May I have your hand?'

'Oh, hang on, you're a fortune teller?' Mel asks. She suddenly relaxes. She's always wanted to go to one but her mum wouldn't let her. This is off tap. She's in the middle of Venice Beach getting her palm read by some witch.

'No, not a fortune teller, I don't believe in them. Let's just say I'm a spiritual liaison.'

'Okay, well, whatever, am I gonna win the comp?' Mel asks, offering her hand. 'Also, I really like this guy, even though I haven't technically met him yet. Will we hook up?'

Claudia cradles Mel's hand, closes her eyes and draws in a deep breath, then sits in silence for a few seconds while Mel looks on intently. Finally, Claudia releases a sigh and lightly presses her hands either side of Mel's.

'Melissa, you have a very strong presence. You have the potential to change lives,' she says, then pauses. 'You will fall in mutual love by the end of your journey here on the opposite side of the under. It's with somebody you don't really know, but even that's not all it seems, as you do in fact know them. Your feet are struggling to connect and the only way they truly will is when your eyes and soul are wide open. Only then will you be truly happy.'

'Mel!' A voice calls from outside. 'Mel, where are you?'

'I'm here, I'm coming,' she replies as Claudia releases her hands and slowly stands. 'What do you mean, so I'm going to meet this guy? And do I fall from my board? Do I just need to put on extra wax?'

Claudia walks into the house without responding. Just as she's about to close the door, she says, without turning around, 'All will be perfect.'

#12

'So did her eyes roll back into her head? Was her head spinning?' asks Carolyn.

Mel laughs. 'No, I said it was creepy, not demonic, you little weirdo.'

They're back at Malibu, chatting at their front door while Grace parks the car. After walking around the Venice canals, they had time for a quick look along Abbot Kinney Boulevard, a street known for its shopping, art stores and delicious food. It was a bit more expensive than they expected, so the only thing Mel purchased was a drink bottle with a pineapple pattern. She can't wait to show Salvador. They were supposed to go out to the discount warehouses, but ran out of time and were ordered back to the house by Mr Sampson.

'Weren't you curious about all the surfboards?' Jaspa

asks, fiddling with the shell bracelet she bought. 'Oh, I wish I got to meet her.'

'Jazz, c'mon, it would've freaked you right out. But yeah, the surfboards were the first thing I noticed, but then I just completely blanked about finding out about them.'

'Let's, like, bust out at midnight and hitch back there,' Carolyn blurts.

Mel gasps with an open-mouthed smirk, then grabs Carolyn in a headlock. 'Damn, I love it when you unleash your rebel. But no way in hell. I escaped murder once, I'm not risking it again! Shhh.' Mel releases Carolyn, holds up a hand and listens. 'Don't let Thommo know what I did, he'll flip.' Footsteps approach and Thomas opens the front door.

'Mr Sampson, did you miss us?' Mel asks as they step into the hallway.

'Oh yes, the silence was awfully deafening, Melissa,' he says, holding the door open for Grace.

'I'll do the jokes, thanks,' Mel deadpans as she pulls her Converse off without bothering to untie them and walks into the lounge, then stops short. 'Oh, hey, hi Trudy. I didn't expect to see you here.' Trudy Hardwick is seated at the dining room table with a Macbook Air in front of her.

'Sorry to surprise you girls, but I'm here to talk about the Bikini Collective day. Sit, sit.'

Mel plonks down in the chair closest to Trudy. The afternoon sun shines on her face, and Mel can clearly see the scar that's dented into her cheek. In interviews Trudy calls it a kiss from the Cloudbreak reef in Fiji. Mel can't believe that she continued to surf through the finals to win the event with her face half hanging off, simply stuck together with tape. Now she's got a permanent reminder of how hardcore she is.

'So, I've spoken to Thomas, and he's agreed to let us do the surf day, so long as it doesn't interfere with your competing and your school work, okay?' The girls nod and Trudy opens a spreadsheet. 'Okay, I'm going to handball all the organising to my management team. That way all we need to do is spread the word and participate on the day.'

Mel tilts her chair back on two legs. 'Whoa, that's so generous of you. When will we do it?'

'Well, the best swell for them to finish your comp is going to be over the weekend, so I think Monday is our best shot, given that you leave on Tuesday night.'

Mel's heart sinks. It's too soon to think about going home. How is she going to adjust to Bonita Shores again after all *this*? 'So, what do you need us to do now?'

'I've had a call-out designed, so I was hoping you

could share it with the Bikini Collective group. We can do it now.' She swings the keyboard around to face Mel, who logs on.

'Oh look,' Mel says to Jaspa and Carolyn. 'Girls have been posting pics of us competing here, how mad.' Several photos have been shared on the girls-only page, showing them running to their heats, stretching on the sand – there's even one taken from the beach, looking up at them in the competitor's area. 'Oh, is that what I think it is, Carolyn?' Mel clicks on a photo and zooms in, then bursts out laughing. She's in hysterics, clutching her stomach, while Carolyn leans across the table to see what's so funny.

There, taking up the entire screen, is a photo of Mel and Jaspa seated at the table, laughing, while next to them Carolyn shoves a massive fork full of spaghetti into her mouth. There are traces of tomato sauce on her cheeks, chin and coat collar. 'Crap, has no one ever heard of privacy?' Carolyn grumbles.

'Oh man. It's the – it's the,' Mel buckles over in giggles, then tries again, 'the expression on your face … it's like pure love!' she blurts before wiping her eyes and burying her face in her hands to try and calm herself down.

Carolyn sits back with folded arms. 'Well, it was a pretty sick spag bol.'

Jaspa pulls the laptop over. 'Here, let me help. Trudy, what would you like us to write?'

'Most of it's on the flyer, but you can also say that I'm donating one of my boards as a prize, and the surfers who're helping on the day so far are, me, Nikki James and Gloria.'

'Gloria?' Mel sits up with a start and her smile disappears. 'Gloria Cruz?'

'Yeah,' Trudy says, leaning across the table to read Jaspa's post. 'We have one of the same sponsors here in LA. She's a really interesting person, that one.'

You can say that again, Mel thinks.

#13

Mel sits in silence and scrapes her fingernail over the wax clumped on the deck of her board. She way over-compensated when applying it this morning, and hopes it won't affect the weight going into turns. The water laps against the fibreglass, and the fortune teller's – no, *spiritual liaison*'s – words from yesterday play over in her head. *Why will my feet struggle to connect?* she wonders.

She looks towards the beach. The five-minute yellow panel is being lowered, then the green one is raised to mark the beginning of her heat. She presses her watch to count down from thirty minutes and glances at Gloria. Yep, still in resting bitch face mode. Mel decides to get away from her vibe and paddles down the point. The waves aren't lining up as well today, which means there are a couple of take-off positions to choose from.

She just has to hope the surf God, Huey, sends the sets her way. She closes her eyes and lifts her face to the sky, the sun beaming onto her eyelids, and whispers, 'Pretty please, Huey.'

She sees a whoosh of yellow carve into the top of the wave in front of her. She studies her competitor as water explodes from the tail of her board, then hears the slap of a body falling against the ocean.

An increasing cross-shore wind brushes Mel's cheek as she squirts water in and out of her hand, waiting for her first decent ride. The couple she's had so far have been under five points. She notes the activity around her, who's catching waves, who's falling and who has priority. The commentator announces that in order to progress onto the quarter finals, Mel requires a 4.1 to move into second or a 7.2 to pip Gloria for first place. Surfing in competitions is weird. You're basically not only hoping that you'll do well, but that the other surfers will do terribly. Not that Mel feels particularly bad about that. Gotta do what you gotta do.

A nicely formed bump of ocean soars towards Mel and jacks up to an overhead peak. Just as she's about to swing the nose of her board into the crest of the wave, the surfer in blue paddles furiously past Mel to the inside and simply orders, 'Don't.' It takes a second for what Gloria just did to sink in. Mel watches her swing into the pitch of the lip and tear the wave to shreds all the way down the line. Mel had priority for that wave – why did she let Gloria get the better of her like that?

She shakes the moment out of her shoulders and readies herself for the next opportunity. The second wave in the set is even bigger. Mel lays on her board with her back arched and takes four big strokes. Her pop-up is fast and allows for a rapid ascent into her first re-entry, where she releases her fins and throws her arms behind her in a lay-back snap. In these moments she feels powerful and dynamic. She's not the kind of person who allows other people to stomp over her, no way. The slight push in the wind provides Mel with a series of launch pads to play with each time a section of wave offers itself up for destruction.

On the paddle back out, with only two minutes remaining, Gloria exits off a wave before even finishing it to race Mel to the take-off point, anxious to keep her from getting another high-scoring ride. Mel drops her head and paddles hard, propelling herself forward with each stroke. She's neck and neck with Gloria. Mel's face is strained and stressed. Gloria's, on the other hand, is expressionless, despite the exertion. This rattles Mel.

As the commentator counts down from 10 seconds, a wave presents itself. Mel takes the inside position, but only by a hand's width. She tucks her feet under her body to connect with the wax, but Gloria also takes off, dropping in on Mel. The commentators deliberate the situation over the loudspeaker and rev up the crowd by discussing a possible rivalry and pending penalty. Gloria flicks off the wave with a steely gaze and Mel stands tall in disbelief, riding to shore without doing a turn. The final scores are read out: 'Melissa Appleby, you came in second on a total of 12.8. Gloria Cruz, congratulations, you won that heat on 16.9. You both progress onto the quarter finals.'

As the shore approaches, Mel remains on her board, riding it until she can lazily jump onto the sand. Her leg-rope remains attached and the board flips around in the shallows, pulling at her ankle. She puts her hand on one hip and cocks it to the side, breathing out her anger before walking back to the competition area.

'What the heck happened?' Mel asks Thomas and Jaspa through clenched teeth. 'Why didn't Gloria get an interference on that last wave?'

'Look,' Thomas says, taking Mel's board so she can pull off her competition vest, 'just calm yourself down and then we'll chat about it.' He directs her upstairs and tells Mel to meet him on the couch once she's changed.

She yanks off her wetsuit and slips on a T-shirt and jeans, then walks into the main competitors' area ruffling water from her hair. Thomas hands her a hot chocolate, which she cups in both hands and brings close to her face. 'Man, I was so pissed, she just kept hassling me.'

Thomas pats the seat next to him. 'Sit.' He waits for Mel to take a sip of her hot chocolate, the warm sweetness soothing her mood.

'You both got to your feet slightly after the siren, so that final wave didn't count.' Thomas pauses, noticing that Mel's breath is stilted. 'You know, it doesn't matter – you both got through regardless. But what Gloria did was stupid. A second earlier and she could have been penalised her highest scoring ride and missed out on the quarter finals.'

'So you're not mad at me for chasing her down?'

'No. Well, there did seem to be some unnecessary hassling, but –'

'That was *her*, that was Gloria. I don't know what her frickin' deal is.'

'As I was saying,' Thomas keeps his tone calm, 'I simply want you to learn from Gloria's mistake and think about what energy you reserve for surfing and what you channel into tactics.'

'You've gotta admit though,' Mel smiles over the steam rising from her cup, 'that swing-around take-off I nailed in the dying seconds was pretty epic.'

'It was a very bold and brave move, yes.' Thomas

places his hands on his knees, then stands up. 'You ready? Comp's over for the day, we'll head back to the house for some study time.'

Mel nods reluctantly and collects her surfboards. Just as she's about to put her phone into her backpack, it beeps with a message.

Hola, Pineapple. Party? Party? Yesy? Yesy?

#14

Mel types a message, hits send and then tosses her phone back onto the white shagpile rug she's lying on with Jaspa and Carolyn.

'Who's that you keep texting?' Jaspa asks absently as she flips intently through a textbook.

'Yeah, Sampson's gonna bust you soon – we're meant to be studying.' Carolyn nods towards the kitchen, where Thomas is cooking dinner.

'Salvador,' Mel whispers, her chin propped on one elbow while she types into her laptop with the other hand. 'There's a really good party on tonight at the beach club and they're all trying to convince me to come.'

Jaspa and Carolyn exchange a glance.

'Carolyn, why don't you come with me? It'll be bangin'!' Mel says under her breath.

Jaspa props herself up. 'What about me, am I invisible?'

'Jazz, I asked Carolyn because she'd sneak out with me in a finger click, she does it all the time at home. But would you? Besides, you've spent every night watching movies with Cooper, so I figured that's what you'll be doing.'

Jaspa shrugs and flops back down. 'You're probably right. But neither of you should be sneaking out anyway.'

'Carolyn?' Mel taps her fingertips against each other, raising her eyebrows encouragingly.

'Nah, I'm out. Me be chill tonight too.'

'What? Why? Out of the three of us you're the one who should be cutting sick, seeing as you're not in the comp.'

'Geez, thanks for the reminder.'

'Sorry.'

'If you must know, I think that Salvador guy's a bit of a knob. They just all seem fake as.'

'What? No way, they're all amazing, you just haven't given them a chance. Like, Tiffany, I told you her Mum's that famous actress, yeah? And Susie is the chick from *Boardin*–'

'I know, I know, you've told us a million times.' Carolyn picks up her laptop and sits up on the couch.

'Sheesh,' Mel mumbles to herself. 'Talk about party poopers.' She opens a new tab on her browser and does some more googling on Salvador. His parents are both Mexican, but they immigrated to America in the '80s. His father's a film producer and his mother a real estate agent, and they all live in Beverley Hills, although there was a brief period when his mum moved out to be with a lover and re-evaluate her marriage – according to Wikipedia's 'personal life' section anyway.

Since Mel arrived in LA, she's felt electric, as if at any moment anything could happen. Bonita Shores is beautiful and the waves are amazing, but everyone there always does the same old things. The only place to hang out is the chicken shop or the surf club, unless someone has a house party where the older kids get stupidly drunk, chain-smoke ciggies and talk obnoxious crap. Mel can't imagine what it must be like to be living in LA as an 18 year old who's invited to all the hottest parties, driving around in a Porsche and living in the word's most famous suburb.

Mel hears the table being set and gets up to inspect. 'Wow, dudes. You've made quite the impression.' It's the boys' turn to help with dinner tonight, and they've whipped up a Mexican feast. Mel photographs the spread and sends the picture to Salvador. 'Oh yum,' she says, wiping up a drip of guacamole from the side of the bowl and licking her finger.

'Okay, as a treat, we'll plate up here and then all sit down to watch a movie while we eat,' Thomas says, placing a large bowl of steaming-hot chilli beans on the table.

Everyone scoops a bit of everything onto their plate and walks down the basement stairs into the mini movie theatre. They take a seat and debate what to watch.

'My vote's for *Stranger Things*,' says Tyler.

'Yeah,' agree the rest of the guys.

Jaspa shakes her head. 'Ooh, that's way too scary!' Cooper smiles and scruffs her hair.

Mel holds her fork in the air. '*13 Reasons Why*.'

'Lame,' Tyler mumbles.

'Dude, it's actually pretty good,' Wil says.

Thomas holds the remote and flips through Netflix. 'I've made an executive decision. Because we're all here as a sporting team, I thought we'd watch,' he pauses while he finds the movie to play, '*Dodgeball*.'

'Nice work, Mr Sampson!' Mel shouts over the hoots and whistles.

The sound of crunching taco shells is drowned out by the movie's opening scene.

Mel texts Salvador throughout the film the last

exchange being:

> *Whose* Dodgeball *side would you be on: the beau-*
> *tiful mean losers, or the ugly underdogs who win?*
> *Oh, darling, I would be on the winning side but*
> *give the ugly underdogs a makeover!*

Mel laughs to herself as the final credits roll. Some people are snoring softly, but everyone starts stirring when Thomas flicks on the lights.

'That movie's so old, but it's still gold,' Mel says, stretching.

'Right, it's nearly nine – off to bed, you lot. Just take your plates to the kitchen, rinse them and then pop them in the dishwasher please,' Thomas says, shutting down the TV. 'I'll wash up the pots.'

'What's the forecast for tomozza?' Mel asks as she follows Thomas to the kitchen.

'Onshore winds,' he says, testing the hot water with his finger. 'I doubt the contest will be on tomorrow, but get some rest regardless, because if it's not, it'll be a study and training day.'

Mel takes the stairs two at a time and opens their bedroom door. Jaspa and Carolyn are already in their pyjamas, brushing their teeth.

'Oh, look at you good girls!' Mel pulls out her

toothbrush, squeezes a dollop of toothpaste onto it and walks into the en suite. 'Thommo seb we robly no surpin tommo,' she says around a mouthful of paste.

Jaspa and Carolyn give her a quizzical look as they spit into the sink and rinse their mouths. 'Err, what was that?' Jaspa giggles.

Mel spits, bends down to rinse her mouth, then tries again. 'Thommo said we're probably not surfing tomorrow.' She wipes a towel across her chin then flicks it at Carolyn's bum. 'The forecast is onshore, so I'm anticipating a sleep-in, yew!'

'That sounds like heaven. Night, girls,' Jaspa says as they all hop into their beds. She switches off the lamp.

'Night, chicks. Well done for getting into the quarters, you two.'

'Thanks Carolyn,' Mel says. 'Well done for being a ripper who'll kick ass at the next comp.'

The room quietens and Mel snuggles under her doona, still in her jeans and jumper. She can make out the faint sound of music playing from the beach club, but she's feeling pretty tired. Salvador sends her a series of videos in an attempt to entice her to join the fun. Him sitting in the heated pool on a blow-up pineapple. Him dancing around the garden with glowsticks, wearing a tutu. Mel's just about to drift off to sleep when another message comes through:

Pineapple, this picture would be even more exquisite with you in it. What are you waiting for, darling? YOLO!!!!

Mel yawns and looks at the photo. It's a selfie of Salvador with a bunch of his friends. Her sleepy eyes linger on the screen for a moment and then widen. She zooms in. There he is, in the back of the group. It's Corey Swain.

She quietly slides out of bed, puts on her sneakers and jacket, tucks her phone into her back pocket and takes a spare leg-rope out of her bag. She unlocks the balcony door and eases it open, the cool night air awakening her cheeks. The north end of the balcony joins the side of the house next to the garden fence. Mel wraps the leg-rope strap around the balcony railing and pulls to check its tightness, then uses the cord to ease herself down, stepping carefully against the wall until she reaches the ground. The backyard is pitch dark, and the house is in complete darkness. As she tiptoes towards the beach walkway the patio light comes on, triggered by a sensor. Mel bolts over the grass, past the pool and scurries down the steps without looking behind her.

#15

Mel eases herself down to the walkway and continues up the beach towards the music and laughter. Her pace slows as she nears the secret side door, and her tummy starts to churn. What if Vincent isn't there to let her in this time? She doesn't want to stand there like a loser, or try to get in and be turned away. There are no more messages from Salvador yet. Perhaps she should just wait.

She leans against the fence and scrolls through her phone, trying to look busy. If only Jaspa and Carolyn were here. Mel considers turning back and going home. She's used to being a known personality in a small country town. She's been on the front page of the local paper and interviewed for community radio shows – there's not one person in Bonita Shores who doesn't know her name. But in this moment, right now, she feels like a small fish that nobody in this big pond cares about.

A young couple walk around the corner up to the gate and push a bell Mel didn't know was there. They smile at her as Vincent opens the door. Deciding it's now or never, Mel gives Vincent a nod hello and follows them through. She's in!

Taking a deep breath, she wanders through the garden, which is lit up with flashing fairy lights and rows of candles. She hovers near a tree and scans the crowd for Salvador. He's hard to miss, dancing in the booth next to the DJ, wearing oversized novelty sunglasses and a spotted long-sleeved shirt tucked messily into tight black ankle-freezer jeans. She gives him a big wave and he comes bouncing over.

'Pineapple! How long have you been here? Did you bust out of surfer prison?' He takes both her hands and see-saws them from side to side in a little dance.

Mel snickers. 'Yeah, I abseiled off the balcony. I can only stay for an hour.'

'Well then,' Salvador calls over a waitress, picks up two cups and thrusts one into Mel's hand, 'drink up, darling. We've got a lot of party ground to cover in one hour.'

She follows him to the dance floor and they dance

while gulping their drinks. Mel shudders at how strong it is and decides to take smaller sips. She looks down at her jeans and jumper and suddenly feels underdressed. All around her there's tons of bling – skimpy sequinned tops, stiletto heels and the odd pair of white pants.

She spies Susie leaning against the fence, smiling intently at a guy wearing a leather jacket, his dark hair brushed forward. Mel can't see his face, but she can tell who it is. Her heart sinks as Corey reaches behind Susie's head and guides her in to greet his lips. Mel stares, motionless, as everyone dances around her. Susie mouths something funny and as Corey laughs and turns his head, a trickle of euphoria flows through Mel and she releases a giddy sigh. It's not Corey after all.

A familiar Daft Punk guitar riff comes bursting through the speakers, and the crowd cheers and rushes for the dance floor. As Pharrell Williams' voice oozes into the song, Salvador encourages Mel to mimic his '80s-inspired moves, and throughout the chorus over fifty voices can be heard screaming about getting lucky.

'This is so nuts, thanks for inviting me,' Mel yells over the music, raising her hands in the air. 'I may never leave!'

'Yes, yes, stay here and you can live in my basement – that's not half as creepy as it sounds – and you can take me surfing and we'll write a sitcom about the

Aussie who comes to LA to be with her bestie, which is obviously me.' Salvador takes a deep breath and then swigs the rest of his drink in one gulp, most of it dripping down his chin.

'What's the deal with school, do you go?' Mel asks, picking up the cup Salvador threw on the ground and putting it in a bin.

'Well, I've been expelled from two schools and didn't graduate, so I'm under the very flexible thumb of home schooling this year.'

'Oh, a bit like me,' Mel says. 'Well, we go to a school that's for athletes and then all study on the road when we're competing. This is my first big trip away without my folks.'

'And how are you enjoying the splendidness of sweet, sweet freedom?' Salvador whirls around with his hands in the air.

'What do you think?' Mel grins and starts jumping up and down to the beat of the next banger.

'I think you fit right in, Pineapple.'

Mel spies a crowd of people gathered by the palm trees. 'Oh, it's limbo, come on, come on!' She grabs Salvador by the arm.

Salvador pushes straight to the front of the line, pinches his jeans at the thigh to pull them up, and then arches his back and just makes it under the pole. Mel claps, and when it's her turn she easily backbends to the other side. Salvador struggles through his next turn and falls flat on his back when he can't quite get his belly underneath the bar. As more people are eliminated, the pole gets lower and lower. When Mel swans up for her next turn it's only at knee height. Salvador starts a chant of 'Pineapple, Pineapple' and everyone around them joins in.

Mel rips off her shoes and throws them to Salvador. While doing a little hand jive to the music, she widens her stance, squats low and shuffles on the inner edges of each foot towards the pole. Once it reaches her chest, she engages her core, leans back and keeps inching her way to the other side. When she's almost through, she tilts her head as far back as it'll go, her hair brushing against the grass, and with strength and control exits and pulls her body up to stand. Screams and clapping can be heard around her – she's the winner. As her eyes regain focus she realises that standing right in front of her, clapping with a beaming smile and dreamy eyes, is Corey Swain.

'That's quite the skill you have,' he remarks, while lightly scratching the top of his head. Mel's not sure if it's to relieve an itch or show off his bicep tattoo.

She tries to keep her cool. 'Yeah, I knew being the Australian limbo champ would come in handy.'

'What? You're not? That's awesome.'

Mel loves how he emphasises that last word, it sounds so American. 'No, I'm definitely kidding. Although it might be my back-up plan if the whole surfing thing falls through.'

'Oh, wow. So are you here for that competition at the pier?'

Mel studies his pixie-like appearance, with his prominent cheekbones narrowing down to his chin. She's never met a guy who looks like this – tattoos, leather jacket, dark hair, pale skin – like he's from some kind of grungy underground scene. 'Yeah, I'm here with the Australian team.'

'Well, I do love surfer girls.'

Mel smiles at this news, exposing the tiny gap between her front teeth.

Salvador walks over and hands Mel another drink. 'There's only so much beauty I can handle in such a confined space. Have you two met?'

'Well, not really –', they begin to say together.

'I'm Corey,' he says, holding his hand towards Mel.

Mel takes it and snickers. 'Pleasure to meet you. And I'm Mel.' His hand is warm, and the handshake lingers. She takes a nervous sip from her cup. 'How do you two know each other?'

Salvador leans on her shoulder and points towards

Corey. 'Well, we were in junior high together until I, let's say, "got moved".' He uses his fingers to form air quotes, then continues. 'But now Papa owns the gallery space that Corey works from. He's quite the famous arteest.'

'Oh, you are? That's so cool,' Mel says, pretending she hasn't spent many hours snooping on Google. 'What's your art like?'

'Apparently mixed media collage. I don't really know what to call it, to be honest.' He picks up his jacket from the base of the tree and slips it on, looking like he's just stepped out of a music video clip. 'Alright guys, I'm going to bail. I've got a shoot in the morning.'

Mel looks at her phone. Crap, it's almost 1 am. 'I really have to go too.'

Salvador sticks his bottom lip out. 'Oh, but this party will suck without you two.'

'You know it won't,' Mel says, draining her cup and putting on her shoes.

'Yes you're right, it totally won't. But that doesn't mean I won't miss you.' Salvador embraces them both together, then calls across the yard through his hands. 'Tiffany! Get that booty on the dance floor this minute!'

Corey laughs. 'Do you need a ride anywhere?'

'I'm fine. I'm staying just two houses that way.' She

points, then swings her arm in the opposite direction. 'Oops, I mean that way.'

'I can walk you home if you like?'

'Oh, that's cool, I'll be fine, it's not far.' *Dammit, what are you thinking? Who cares how far it is!*

'Are you sure? It's pretty dark.'

'Well, if you don't mind. Thanks.'

They walk side by side along the narrow walkway. As they near the steps to the house, Mel's arm brushes against his. She wonders if they'll make out. If they do it'll have to be at the beach or by the pool. But she really has to get back to bed before anyone realises she's missing.

'Well, this is me,' she says, the onshore wind whipping her hair all over her face.

'Cool. It was really lovely to meet you. I hope I get to see you again.'

This must be it. She stands on the spot with a nervous grin. Will he hug her first and then go in for the kiss? Or perhaps he's the more passionate type and will launch right in and go straight for the mouth. As she subtly moistens her lips, he picks up her hand and brings it to his mouth, then jumps down onto the sand and walks away.

Mel lingers for a moment, raising her face to the wind and allowing the ocean spray to mist her skin.

Then she creeps tightly along the inside of the fence to avoid setting off the sensor light and waits at the bottom of the balcony for a moment to steady her head. She's not sure if she's dizzy from the drinks or because she's just met the love of her life.

The leg-rope taps against the wall in the breeze. She'll have to be quick – the patio light will turn on the moment she leaves the fence. Launching herself at the cord, she scurries her way up, unwraps the leash, eases through the balcony door and slips straight under the covers, with a grin on her face and Daft Punk's groove still bouncing in her head as she slips off to sleep.

#16

'Mel! Hey, Mel wake up!'

Someone's hand is on her shoulder, shaking her back and forth. Their words amplify the pain throbbing against her skull. She silently wishes whoever it is would please take their morning enthusiasm down a notch or suffer the consequences. She tries to wet her lips, but her mouth is too dry. In her half-asleep daze, she envisages reaching around for her water bottle and taking several long relieving gulps. But in reality she's motionless, too tired to move. Someone opens the curtains. The sunlight penetrates through her closed eyelids and stabs into her brain like a knife laced with headache-inducing poison.

Mel places a pillow over her head. 'Jesus, close the frickin' curtains.'

'Oh, sorry, sure.' Jaspa pulls them back together. 'We're about to have breakfast – Mr Sampson's made American-style waffles. Are you sick?'

Mel realises she's actually *really* hungry. Now she can't think of anything *but* waffles. A sweet aroma wafts up from the kitchen and teases the emptiness in her stomach. She's sure waffles will help relieve her urge to vomit.

'You go, Jazz. I'll be down in a sec,' she croaks.

Mel waits for Jaspa to leave, then closes her eyes for a few more seconds before sitting up. She waits for her head to steady and for the room to stop spinning, then stumbles to the bathroom to splash cold water on her face. The sound of cutlery scraping against plates grows louder as she descends the stairs.

'Nice of you to join us, Melissa.' Thomas motions to the only spare seat. 'Is everything okay?'

Mel looks at all the people seated around the table, the volume of conversation growing as they try to talk over each other. She feels overwhelmed as she makes her way to her chair. 'I'm just feeling a little off today. Probably a virus or something.' She pitches her fork into the stack of waffles and puts one on her plate, then smothers it in maple syrup. She cuts off a corner and pops it into her mouth, chewing slowly before making the commitment to swallow. Her stomach muscles spasm, but she breathes slowly to calm them down, then takes another bite. She looks up to see Carolyn staring at her from across the table.

'What?' Mel asks defensively before putting her fork down. She doesn't think she can eat any more.

Carolyn narrows her eyes. 'So you're sick, huh?' She leans forward to whisper. 'That doesn't have anything to do with sneaking in this morning and waking up in your clothes, does it?'

'Shhh!' Mel widens her eyes and places a finger to her lips. 'Jesus, shut up.'

Carolyn spears a waffle and holds her fork in the air. 'You know I'll torture the details out of you.' She shoves the entire waffle into her mouth with a smirk.

'What details?' Jaspa breaks away from her conversation with Cooper to lean in towards the girls.

'Nothing. No details. Just everyone enjoy your breakfast and shut the heck up. My god you're a nosy bunch.' Mel slumps back to move her food around the plate, then stands. 'Mr Sampson, I'm going back upstairs to lie down.'

'Do you need anything? Should I take you to the doctor?'

'Nah, I'll be fine.' She glares at Carolyn. 'I'll just have a quick rest.'

'Well, the contest is off for the day. But we might go and find some waves if you're up to it.'

'Okay, I'll see.'

'Oh, you'll be up to it,' Carolyn jumps in with a tease. 'And don't forget it's also a study day.'

Mel tightens her mouth, willing Carolyn to shut hers, and walks upstairs. She flops onto the bed and pulls the doona up to her neck, then lets her mind wander back to last night. The dancing. The outfits. And oh my god, the limbo. Plus of course, Corey kissed her. Sure, it was on the hand, but at least it was *somewhere*. That definitely counts as kissing.

* * *

'That so doesn't count as kissing,' Carolyn says after Mel tells them everything.

'I think it does,' Jaspa says dreamily. 'It's even more romantic than actual kissing.' She looks up at the ceiling and releases a pleasant sigh, her hand on her heart.

'See!' Mel groans and lies back down on her pillow, her hand to her forehead.

'But I still don't think you should be sneaking out like that.' Jaspa plays with her hair, plaiting it over her shoulder. 'You're always the one saying we should be serious about surfing.'

'I *am*.' Mel tries not to think about all the times she's grilled Jaspa for being too vague in competitions or not tactical enough. 'I knew we wouldn't be on today, so just relax.'

'You just seem a bit,' Jaspa pauses and bites her bottom lip, 'distracted. And you don't even usually drink,' she adds.

'Jesus, sue me for trying to have a bit of fun.'

'Yo, don't be a bitch to Jaspa just cos you've ruined yourself,' Carolyn cuts in, getting up off Mel's bed.

A knock at the door interrupts them. Mel rolls over to face the wall. 'Can't everyone just leave me the heck alone?'

'Girls, may I come in?' Thomas asks from the hallway.

'Enter,' Carolyn bellows as she fumbles through her bag for socks.

Thomas leans against the door. 'We're all jumping in the van to surf up the coast. Be ready in thirty?'

'Oh goodie, a road trip!' Jaspa claps her hands and bounces on the bed until Mel mumbles for her to stop before she throws up.

Thomas shoves his hands into his pockets and walks into the room. 'Mel, will you be joining us, or do you want to stay home to rest?'

'Oh, she'll be joining us alright,' Carolyn says without looking up.

'Yes, I'll be there,' Mel says through the back of her head. 'I just need a bit more beauty sleep.' She waits until she hears Thomas walk out and close the door behind him, then mumbles to Carolyn without turning over. 'Little rat. I'll get you back one day.'

* * *

Mel stirs as they pull up at the beach. The dream of her and Corey escaping the party to walk arm-in-arm along the beach, of him stroking back her hair and pressing his lips against hers, fades as she drifts into consciousness. She lifts her head to see she's been asleep on Wil's shoulder and left a tiny patch of dribble on his T-shirt.

'Why didn't you push me off?' Mel croaks, catching her reflection in the rear-view mirror. She wipes her sleeve across her mouth, then reaches up and pats down her matted hair.

'You looked kinda cute and peaceful,' Wil says. 'I figured it was best not to stir the beast.'

'Yeah, well, now I'm stirred, so watch out for my bite.' Mel snaps her teeth at him, then follows the others out of the van.

Despite the wind, the surf looks quite fun, with several a-frame peaks rising up and down the beach. Surfers scatter the line-up like chocolate chips on a cookie. Mel suddenly has an urgent need to submerge into the ocean. Each peeling wave beckons her, promising to make her feel better, and to not judge her for what she did the night before. She pulls her wetsuit on and the noise of several boards being waxed echoes around her like an orchestra, triggering the anticipation of catching that first wave.

Her feet navigate the rocks as she reaches the shore, the ocean lapping up to her toes to awaken her whole body. The water's chilly, but the sun burns into her black wetsuit and sends tingles across her skin. Mel sees the others stretching, so flops her body to bend lazily over her thighs and clasps her hands behind her back. That will have to do – it's all she can manage. She rises and waits a moment to steady her scattered head, then launches her board into the ocean. As the water rolls over her it feels like she's eaten a bowl of ice-cream too quickly, and her head protests in pain. But after a few minutes her mind is clear and her eyes alert.

A bump of water rises in front of her, so Mel paddles for the wave, calling to Carolyn to take the left while she goes right. The ocean lifts Mel into a clean drop. Her tummy flips with excitement as a section dares her to try something new. She leans into the bottom of the wave, but her rise to the crest is sluggish, her legs unable to produce the speed they usually would. She wraps a turn into the top of the wave, but mistimes and is smacked down into the breaking foam. As she's tumbled around underneath the turbulence, she surrenders and humbly accepts that Mother Nature is going to kick her butt back into shape. Once she pops up, she takes in a deep breath and pulls her board towards her. A couple of waves push her back before she gathers the strength to paddle to Carolyn.

'Hey,' she says, sitting upright and collecting her breath. 'Thanks for dogging me into coming surfing. This is actually the best thing ever.'

#17

Mel's phone buzzes. She takes it back out of the locker and sees the words 'Mother Dearest' lighting up the screen. Her finger hovers over the red phone icon for a moment, but then she presses the green and brings the phone to her ear.

'Ma, how's it goin'? I know, I know, sorry I haven't buzzed you back. Yeah, great. I'm just about to surf the quarters, I'm in my smelly wetsuit as we speak. Yep, Jazz is in the fourth quarter but Carolyn's already knocked out. I know, bummer. I'm great, I totally love it here. Mrs Rogers from the back said what? Nah, it's not dangerous. But how would she even know? Mum … Mum … Mum, listen, I don't really give a rats what Mrs Rogers says. What's Dad shouting in the background?

Jesus, tell him to make his own breakfast. He shouldn't talk to you like that. Okay, Mum … Mum … MUM, I can't have this convo now with you riling on each other. I've gotta go, I'm about to surf. Thanks. Yes, okay. I said okay, I promise I'll call. Okay, bye.'

Mel stares at the phone for a moment before putting it back in her locker. If there's a picture of how Mel doesn't want to live her life, it's her parents. Sometimes she wonders if they even like each other. Her skin becomes clammy and the tightness of her wetsuit starts to irritate her. She sits down and pulls the neck of her wetsuit out with two fingers to let in some air. Her heartbeat taps rapidly against her ribs and she struggles to steady her breathing.

'Hey, are you okay?' Jaspa stands at the bench with her surfboard under her arm, her wetsuit draped over it.

'Yeah. I just spoke to Mum.' Mel draws in a deep breath and shakes her shoulders.

'Oh.' Jaspa puts her board in the rack and sits next to Mel. 'How is she?' Jaspa has been in the firing line between Mel and her mum many a time.

'She's, you know, okay. She says good luck, by the way.'

'Oh, that's sweet. Mum says the same to you.'

'She just does my head in.' Mel leans her head back

against the wall. 'I don't care one smidgen about Mrs Rogers or any Bonita Shores gossip. And Dad was being a dick, as usual. Our town sucks.'

Jaspa furrows her brow. 'No, you know that's not true. We're so lucky to live there. Right on the beach, beautiful forest, we see each other every day …'

'Huh, yeah right. We *used* to, before loverboy hijacked the scene.' Mel gets up, slams her locker shut and pulls her surfboard from the rack. She can see that Jaspa is trying to work out what to say, but Mel doesn't give her the chance. 'My quarter's on. I'll see you after yours. Good luck.' She takes the stairs two at a time and collects her competition vest. They've given her green, her least favourite colour. Why would anyone like a colour that looks like snot?

As she turns from the check-in counter she almost bumps into Gloria, who just grunts in annoyance and swerves around her. *Jesus*, Mel thinks. *What is her problem?* She tries to work out if they've ever met before this contest. Maybe Mel made a smartassed comment online or something? She shrugs and heads for the shore.

Three other competitors join Mel on the walk up the beach. The wind swung offshore overnight and, as predicted, the swell has risen considerably. A storm far out to sea releases energy that steams into the shallower waters like a train to wrap waves around the point in parallel lines. Mel puts her board on the sand and squats up and down, swivelling and reaching behind her on each rise to mimic a cutback. Rising to her feet, she taps the leg-rope strap against her shin to release the sand and then attaches it to her right ankle. Pumping her shoulders up and down, she thinks, *this is it*. This is her goal, her way out of her mundane existence: become a World Junior Champion in her first year on tour.

The commentator announces the five-minute mark, so Mel runs into the shore break and launches onto her board, gliding over a ball of foam. Walls of whitewater push into the paddle-out spot, but Mel strokes hard to combat the current. There's no room to take a breath; if she stops paddling for a moment, she'll be swept down the point and will have to start all over again. Just when Mel is wondering if she has the stamina to get under another set, she realises she's in open water. She takes a moment to gather herself and prepare for the start of her heat. The red brick mansion on the cliff is her line-up point. She swirls her legs underneath her and uses each hand as a rudder to keep in position. The siren sounds, the green board is raised. The quarter final is *on*.

Despite all the waves coming through, the heat gets off to a slow start. Wide, larger sets keep catching them off guard, and their scramble to get underneath the rush of breaking water constantly pushes them out of position. The surfer in white is the first of the four to post a score. Mel watches from the back of the wave as the tip of her board can be seen whipping several sections of water all the way down the line.

When an opportunity finally presents itself, Mel looks around to make sure she has a clear path to take the wave, then launches herself forward. After just four strokes, she's picked up quicker than expected and thrown forward with the pitch of the wave. In a scurry, she lands her feet on the deck while in mid-air, her stomach dropping.

She lands safely with a satisfying thud, but as she leans to slice her rail through the blue her back foot slips, and she slaps hard against the ocean. The chaos of breaking water pulls her under, and while she allows her body to go limp to save her energy, she realises something feels different. She reaches down and discovers that her leg-rope has snapped, and there is no longer a board attached to it. As soon as she surfaces she looks around frantically and spies her board flipping its way towards the sand, solo. Mel power swims towards the beach. As she reaches her runaway board, she spies Carolyn sprinting towards her.

'Dammit, thanks,' Mel says, taking the new leg-rope

from Carolyn and swapping it with her broken one. 'I've totally blown it.' Her eyes begin to well up and her words catch in her throat.

'Dude, you've still got ten minutes.' Carolyn picks up the board, shoves it under Mel's arm and slaps her on the back. 'Go forth and dominate. Isn't that what you always say?'

Mel lets out a growl and runs up the beach, waving to Carolyn without turning. A brief lull in sets makes her paddle-out easier this time and she quickly reaches her competitors, who wait patiently with priority.

'What happened to you?' asks the surfer in blue over the sound of the ocean.

'Snapped leggie,' Mel replies with a grimace.

'You're Mel from Australia, yeah?'

Mel nods. She looks out to the horizon, waiting for a chance to get back into the heat.

The surfer in blue turns to the other surfer and whispers, 'That's the one, you know, that Gloria …' she trails off when Mel glances their way.

Mel lowers her head and takes a deep breath.

'Surfers in the water, there are two minutes remaining. Green, you require a combination score of 11.2 to move into second place, and red, you require a 6.5. This is a close race, folks.' The commentator's comment bellows out to sea and then echoes through the Malibu mountains.

Mel notices the familiar change of colour in the ocean that happens when a set approaches. The two competitors to her right have priority and are ready to swoop. To her left, the surfer in white is still making her way back out after her last ride. Mel puts a bit of distance between herself and the others. It's a long shot – she needs two scores to progress – but not impossible. She slowly strokes into a wave, keeping an eye on the surfer next to her to see if she'll use her priority to take it. Mel has only a second to make a decision. One more paddle and she'll be into the ride, but risks being penalised for an interference on the other surfer.

To Mel's surprise, out the corner of her eye she spies the surfer in red sharply pulling back her board, giving her the green light. Mel scrambles her arms through the moving water and glides her feet onto the board, dropping down the face with a carpet of blue stretched out before her. Her feet drive into the wax, carving the rail through the ocean, exposing the fins and creating a wake of water behind her. The nose of her board soars up into the pitching lip. She stomps on her back foot and drops her shoulder to soar into a layback snap, sending a spurt of water sky high. Her front foot slides slightly forward and she uses it to gather speed for the next section, swooping into a perfectly-timed cutback from the face of the wave, transitioning up into the wall of foam. As she continues to ride to shore, soaring over flat spots and tagging any sections that stand in her way, she hears the siren sound. Her shoulders slump. The heat is over. The event, for her, is over.

#18

'I don't wanna talk about it.' Mel walks out of the locker room and into the lounge area, running a comb through her wet hair. She scored an 8.8 on her final ride, but didn't have enough time to catch another. There's not really anything left to discuss, but that doesn't stop Thomas and Carolyn from trailing her anyway.

'Seriously, have you guys heard of personal space?'

'Mel.' Thomas sits on a stool opposite her and clasps his hands on the table. 'You did your best. Getting to the quarter finals is incredible.'

Yeah, but winning the event would be so much better, Mel thinks.

'And you did an equipment check. What more could you do?' Carolyn shuffles uncomfortably, her voice pitching a little too high. She's not used to giving pep talks – that's usually Jaspa and Mel's bag.

Mel nods, wondering if she checked her leg-rope before paddling out. She's not entirely sure. Her head is still scattered from the other night.

Thomas continues, despite Mel's efforts to feign disinterest. 'Every heat you surf is a lesson. This is your first year on tour. Just take it wave by wave, okay?'

Mel's phone buzzes in her hand, and she discreetly glances at it. There's a message from Salvador.

Pineapple! I have a free ticket in my sweaty, pudgy hands for you to come and see Double Denim!!!!! It's an afternoon show, so you can get back to surf prison at a decent hour, although I can't promise what my definition of decent is. Say yes and we'll detour the limo. No FOMO, say YES!!!!

The next message is a picture of him and Corey posing in the back of the limousine, draped across the black leather bench seats and doing duck face at the camera.

'Okay, Mel?' Thomas's brows are raised so high it looks like they're about to spring from his forehead.

'What? Ah, yes okay.' Mel rubs her tummy. 'Actually, I'm not feeling so well. Is it okay if I go home to bed?'

'Well, yes. But Jaspa's about to surf, and then they're starting the boys, with Cooper first heat. Don't you want to watch?'

'I do, but she'll understand.' Mel rises lazily from her stool, crinkling her face as though even the slightest movement is too much to bear. She avoids eye contact with Carolyn. 'I just need a really big rest. I think I still have that virus. I wouldn't want to spread it around.'

'You rest up and we'll be back by dinnertime. Just drop me a message when you reach home, please.'

'Will do. I'll be crossing my fingers for Jaspa under the covers,' Mel says, folding her middle finger over her index finger and waving them in the air. She catches Carolyn rolling her eyes, so scurries away, reminding herself not to move too quickly, or she'll give herself away. Once she's down the stairs and on the beach, she replies to Salvador.

OMG YES!!!! Give me 30 minutes.

Nobody is home. Perfect. She texts Thomas to say she's arrived safely, then piles a bunch of cushions underneath her doona. She positions her pyjama top so it's barely visible under the covers, near the pillow, but decides it needs puffing out, so she stuffs the arms full of clothes. It's a bit lame, but should be okay with the lights off. Besides, it's just a precaution, in case Thomas decides to check on her.

Now, what to wear to a music festival? She peels off her leggings and puts on her favourite high-waisted skinny Lee jeans with black ankle boots and a white cropped tank top. Her hair could do with some styling but there's no time for that, so she snatches Carolyn's fedora from the bed, stuffs her phone, money and lip balm into her shoulder bag, rubs a smudge of eyeliner over her lids and grabs her black vinyl jacket. She pauses at the mirror and does a slow turn. Definitely Double Denim worthy.

She pokes her head around the bedroom door and listens. Everyone still seems to be out. She shuffles down the stairs and clip-clops her way up the hallway before glancing outside to see if the coast is clear. The limousine is parked on the road out front. As she sprints towards it the back door opens and she hurls herself inside, giggling as she lands on the floor. She looks up to see Salvador wearing a gold sequinned waistcoat over a light purple T-shirt and black-rimmed Ray Ban aviators with his hair greased back.

'That was quite the entrance, Pineapple. Driver,'

Salvador says, pressing an intercom button, 'you may now take us to rock heaven.'

'That's quite the outfit, Salvador,' Mel responds as she flops down next to him on the long high-backed couch. The walls of the limousine are covered in leopard print, and a red neon bar sits behind the front seats, full of drinks, glasses and nibbles. She smiles at Corey, who's sitting on the opposite side of the limo. He's wearing ripped denim jeans with a Fleetwood Mac T-shirt. Jaspa's dad is always playing Fleetwood Mac on his record player and singing about going his own way, or something. Corey looks younger than Mel remembers, and it takes her a moment to figure out that he's shaved. He winks at her and she blushes with a wide grin.

'So, how'd you go today, surfer girl?' Corey's voice is smooth and his accent lingers on the r's and y's. It gives Mel pleasant prickles all over her body.

She rests her head against Salvador's shoulder and audibly sighs. 'My surfboard decided to do a runner without me, all the way to the shore. A snapped leggie.'

'A snapped *whattie*?' Salvador squeals while moving towards the bar.

'A leggie!' Mel laughs and taps her ankle. 'A leg-rope, the thing that attaches you to your board.'

'Oh, of course I know that. I'm totally down with

surfer dude speak. Beverage?' He holds out a bottle for Mel, who shakes her head.

'Nup, I'm done, no drinking for me today. Can I scab some chips though?'

'Good god, can you *what* some chips?'

Mel giggles. 'Scab. You know, like, not like stealing but taking something of someone's.' She reaches over and grabs a packet of salt and vinegar chips. 'See? I'm a scab.'

Corey grins, revealing a subtle dimple etched in his chin. 'So, do you know Double Denim, Mel?' His words float towards her like a waterfall of hot chocolate, cascading over her.

She crunches quickly then swallows. 'Yes, I love them, they're kickass.' She licks the salt from her fingers, then discreetly wipes them on her jeans.

'Well, my little pineapple, you're going to see their kickassness from,' Salvador pulls something from his pocket and throws it towards Mel, 'backstage!'

A laminated pass attached to a lanyard lands in Mel's lap. She picks it up with an open-mouthed gasp. 'What? Oh my god, thank you so, so much, this is insane!' She places the lanyard over her neck and holds up the pass, which says 'Friend of Double Denim' on the front and 'AAA' on the back. She hugs it tightly to her chest and grins. 'I will never forget this, Salvador.'

She takes her phone out of her bag, holds up the pass and takes a selfie, then types a quick message to Jaspa.

I'm so sry I didn't stick around to watch your heat but THIS just happened. You understand, yeah? Pls cover for me. I told Thommo I was sick so just stall him and say I'm sleeping. I'll sneak back in just after dark if you can attach my leggie to the balcony pretty pls. Tell Carolyn too. LOVE you!!!! xxxxx

Mel shoves her phone back into her bag and joins Salvador in singing the chorus to Double Denim's 'Sunny Daze'. She doesn't notice Jaspa's reply blinking on the screen, the text unable to translate the emotion.

Oh, sure thing. You're so lucky! By the way, in case you'd like to know, I won my quarter today, in the semis tomorrow. x

#19

Mel leans over the railing of the raised VIP platform. Thousands of people are laughing, dancing and singing as the Californian sun beams through the surrounding palm trees, showering the crowd with light. People wear T-shirts with hand-scrawled statements like 'Smart is the new pretty' and 'I throw like a girl, what of it?'. In front of the stage, Mel spies a group of teenagers who are all dressed in denim jackets and jeans, wearing red bandanas around their hair. They look amazing. Mel takes a photo and makes a mental note to try that style back home. Down below, a guy waves to get Mel's attention.

He cups his hands around his mouth and calls to her. 'How did you get that spot? Are you someone famous?'

Mel shakes her head with a laugh. 'No,' she shouts down. 'I'm just with these guys.'

Salvador leans over her shoulder and declares: 'This is Pineapple, and she's the best surfer in the worrrrrrrrrld!'

An expression of awe forms on the guy's face and Mel pulls back, laughing, and playfully slapping Salvador on the arm. She had to admit, what he said felt pretty good. She could get used to this.

A chant of 'Double Denim' starts from the crowd, willing the band to make an appearance. The DJ turns down the music, and the anticipation builds. Mel feels tingles of excitement spreading throughout her body. The stage remains empty, but the fret-crawling riff to 'Summer Blue' blasts through the speakers, prompting a roar from the crowd. After a few seconds, the drummer walks onto the stage wearing ankle-freezer flares and a sleeveless denim jacket. She claps her drumsticks in the air before sitting behind her kit and tapping the snare drum. She's followed by the bass player and keyboardist, who take their positions on opposite sides of the stage and begin to play.

Mel can barely contain the feelings bundled up inside her. That familiar melody she's punished her parents with from behind her bedroom door is now playing out live right in front of her. As she scans the stage for the guitarist, Lauren McDonald finally struts slowly to the front of the stage and everyone squeals. She's playing a cherry red hollowbody Epiphone that's slung across her chest, suspended by a black leather guitar strap with a silver lightning bolt down the centre. Her denim jumpsuit starts with a boobtube top and tapers down to skinny zipped legs, and her left arm is covered in flower tattoos.

'How you doin', Santa Monica?' Lauren says, leaning into the microphone and looking over the top of the crowd. 'I gotta tell ya, it's good to be home, yeow!' The bass drum kicks in and all the instruments follow, lifting the crowd into elation. Lauren launches into the first line, and is joined by a sea of voices.

> *'The sun is up, so why am I still down? Hey!*
> *It's like I'm followed by an only cloud. Hey!*
> *As an FYI, my summer is a different shade of blue*
> *to yooooooou.'*

Mel feels the entire platform shake under stomping feet, and an electricity of emotion pierces every cell in her body. Her eyes well up – the song means a lot to her – and she can't believe she's here in this moment listening to it live. She stands on her tippy toes and leans over the railing, belting out every lyric as though she wants the whole world to hear.

Corey drapes his arm around Mel's shoulder and smiles down at her.

'So, are you having fun, surfer girl?'

Mel freezes. She's not sure her body, or even her *soul*, can handle much more excitement. She blinks back her tears and her grin widens towards her ears, making her cheeks hurt.

'Corey,' she says, turning to face him, 'this is as much fun as a ten-second barrel.'

#20

'Are you sure they won't mind me coming?' Mel asks, following Salvador through a gate and then underneath the stage scaffolding. They flash their passes at security as they go.

'Darling, of course not! You're now actually surgically attached to my hip, so *not* coming is in fact a medical impossibility.'

She snickers, taking Salvador's hand and slipping her other hand into Corey's as they weave towards another gate, where a security guard ushers them to a large bell tent. A woman ticks off their names and wraps a black band around their wrists, then they walk inside. The interior is quite cosy, perhaps three times the size of Mel's bedroom. A DJ plays old-school tunes like the

Beatles and Blondie, and about thirty people laze around on a scattering of battered couches.

Corey is still holding Mel's hand, and she suddenly feels so adult. She arrived in a limo, got VIP tickets to see Double Denim, is backstage with the band and is linking limbs with the hottest guy in Hollywood.

'Oh Salvador,' someone sings over the sound of music and voices.

Salvador breaks away from Mel and Corey and swans open-armed to a group of people sitting on a red velvet lounge. Lauren stands up to greet him with an embrace, kissing his cheeks. Her jet-black fringe is sharp, dropping down into a neck-length bob, and Mel immediately wants to reinvent her own entire look.

Salvador takes a break from showering Lauren and the band with compliments and calls to Mel. 'Come, come,' he says, waving her over. 'Lauren, I would like you to meet Mel from Australia, who I have adorably nicknamed Pineapple.'

Mel wipes her hands on the back of her jeans, then holds one out to Lauren. 'So great to meet you, that show was mad.'

Lauren leans in to greet Mel, placing a hand on her back and guiding her to sit down. 'Thanks. Please, join us.'

Mel flops onto the couch between Lauren, Corey

and Salvador, smiling as she listens to the conversations carting back and forth around her.

'Oh, oh!' Salvador suddenly springs to the edge of his seat and taps Mel on the knee. 'Let's tell everyone the Aussieisms you taught me the other night! Umm, what was it, a rogan?'

'A bogan,' Mel giggles.

'What's a *bogan*?' Lauren asks.

'Kinda like our rednecks,' Salvador says. 'But generally much more attractive, a tad more tolerable, and tanned.'

Lauren laughs. 'It sounds like a collective noun for boogers if you ask me.' She then turns to Mel. 'So, is this your first time in LA?'

'Yeah, I'm here with the surf team.'

'Surf team?' Lauren repeats.

'Uh huh, for a contest at Malibu.' Mel tries to keep her cool. She can't believe she's talking to *Lauren McDonald*.

'Oh, that is so rad.' Lauren leans forward, resting her hands between her knees and peers from under her fringe. 'You know, I kinda surf as well. When I'm not touring.' She shrugs.

'I thought so.' Mel nods. Her heart's racing, but her body language is relaxed. 'So many of your songs are about the ocean and the coast. I think that's why I love them so much.'

Dammit, does she sound too fangirl stalker? Maybe she should take it down a notch.

'Well thanks, chick.' Lauren picks up the bowl of popcorn from the table, offers some to Mel, then pops a few pieces between her matte red lips. 'How are you enjoying our fine land here?'

'I'm having the best time, I never want to leave,' Mel replies. 'All of this stuff that you guys get to do, this stuff never happens at home.' The most exciting thing that happens in Bonita Shores is the annual fete day fundraiser for the surf club. But there's only so many cupcakes with sprinkles and off-key school orchestras a person can handle.

'Well, just be careful what you wish for. It's not always roses.' Lauren sees someone waving across the room and gets up. 'See what I mean? I've just been summoned for business talk. Urgh.' She rolls her eyes and walks off.

Mel smiles and scans the surroundings. Salvador, Susie and Tiffany are leaning against chairs trying to out-twerk each other, while the rest of the band are playing a game of Jenga with Corey. She spots someone in the corner who she definitely recognises from online, even though she can't quite place them. One day, when she qualifies for the main surf tour, this is what her life could look like, *always*. Surf all day and party all night.

The line to the portaloo has finally died down, so Mel hops up and scurries over. When she returns, a bunch of people are gathered around the couch.

'Okay everyone, listen up!' Lauren leaps onto the table and holds her hands in the air. 'I've got three words to say to you nut jobs. Party at the palace!'

'That's four words!' someone laughs.

'Oh, yeah right, four! If you don't know where it is then you're not invited. Otherwise, see you in the hot tub!' Lauren jumps down and people start following her out of the tent.

Mel gets outside and realises it's starting to get dark. Corey playfully tips her hat forward with his finger, then wraps an arm around her shoulders and pulls her to his side. 'You wanna join us for a bit of fun?'

'Umm.' Mel pulls out her phone and scans the messages from Jaspa. They're mainly just questions or updates: Cooper got knocked out of the contest so she's been consoling him, but Wil and Tyler progressed through. Is she okay and having fun? When will she be home? There's nothing about Mr Sampson being suspicious.

'Oh, you simply *must* come, Pineapple,' Salvador jumps in. 'The palace is Lauren's house in the Hollywood Hills. She has a spa, a light-up dance floor and a pet pig. Where in little ol' Aussie land would you get that, mmm?'

Mel thinks for a moment, and glances down at her phone again. It's only 7 pm. Corey leans into her. His body is warm and he smells like musky honey. She'll get Jaspa to tell Thommo she's still sleeping, so not to bother with dinner. Everyone will go to bed eventually, and then she can sneak back in. That's probably smarter than going home now, while everyone's still awake. Besides, she can't come all the way to LA and not go to Hollywood. That settles it then.

Mel looks up at Corey, then gives Salvador a mischievous smile.

'I'm in.'

#21

'Jaspa, you've got visitors.'

Jaspa moves quickly to the top of the stairs before Thomas comes up. With Carolyn's help, she's managed to convince him that Mel's not hungry and wants to keep sleeping. But Jaspa's a terrible liar, and her insides are in knots – she's terrified she'll blow it. It's not the first time she's had to stretch the truth for Mel. Like the time they spent the day at Bryon Bay when their parents thought they were watching a movie and shopping at the Pacific Grove mall. Jaspa crumbled when her mum innocently asked her what she'd bought at the shops. Jaspa copped a week's grounding and Mel accused her of being an amateur.

'Coming,' Jaspa replies, closing the bedroom door

behind her and heading down the stairs to see Trudy and Gloria sitting with Carolyn at the dining table.

'Oh, hi,' she says, caught completely off guard. She walks over and takes a seat, embarrassed that she's already changed into her pyjamas.

'Sorry to ambush you. It's a bummer Mel's sick, but I wanted to officially introduce you to Gloria,' Trudy places a hand on Gloria's shoulder, 'and fill you in on some more details about the Bikini Collective day.'

'Hi,' Jaspa says warmly to Gloria. 'I've seen you around the contest this week.'

Gloria offers little more than a grunt, so Carolyn jumps in. 'Dude, we've been watching you surf, and it's freakishly next level.'

'Thanks.' Her response is still blunt, but she seems to thaw out a little.

As Trudy lists all the sponsors who are donating prizes and talks about what they can do on the day, Jaspa sits back and listens, twirling her hair around her finger. Her mind wanders. Why does Mel always put her in these positions? Why can't she just be happy sitting around the house in her pyjamas with Jaspa?

Trudy's voice brings her back into the moment.

'Jaspa? Everything sound sweet to you?'

'What? Oh, yes. Yes, that's so amazing, we really appreciate it.' Jaspa gets up to see Trudy and Gloria out.

'I'll fill Mel in on the details.' She's impressed by her own quick thinking. Mel would be proud!

As they walk up the hallway, Jaspa's phone bleeps with another message from Mel – now she's going to the Hollywood Hills. She always pushes things so close to the edge, and expects her friends to be there to catch her.

'Hey, Gloria.' Jaspa touches Gloria's arm while Trudy walks on ahead. 'You're from this area, right?' she whispers.

'Yeah, well, not this exact area,' Gloria deadpans while rubbing her thumb and finger in the air to indicate money. 'But yeah, I'm from LA.'

Jaspa bites her bottom lip and shifts uncomfortably. 'Do you happen to know a Salvador, Susie, Tiffany and Corey?'

'Yep, the Brat Pack. They're trouble.'

#22

The limousine turns into a steep driveway that travels for another 200 metres before they even reach the entrance of the house. Twenty of them pile out of the back seat, some carrying cartons of drink and pizza boxes.

'Let's get this freakin' party started,' someone yells, and everyone hoots in agreement.

As Mel climbs the stairs behind everyone else, she glances back and sees the limousine turn around and drive away. Her stomach flips. How's she going to get home? But above her is Corey's gorgeous, smiling face, and he's beckoning to her. Why waste time thinking about getting home when there's limitless fun to be had? Besides, Salvador knows she can only stay for a couple of hours.

As she nears the house she gasps. The exterior is a stylish light grey and charcoal, with sharp, clean lines. The house is three stories high with enormous wrap-around balconies on the second and third levels. One wall is completely covered with plants, and perched on the cliff is an infinity pool and a spa almost the size of Mel's entire backyard.

'Are you kidding me?' Mel steps up onto the sprawling patio, where she's greeted by an endless sea of lights spanning across Los Angeles. She's overcome by a surge of adrenaline. She couldn't be further from Bonita Shores than she is right at this moment. There must be a million homes below her, and she bets every one of them has an exciting story.

Her arms fly open and she twirls around, feeling the cool night air brushing over her cheeks. 'Hello, Hollywood!' she calls out towards the sky.

'Hello, Pineapple,' Salvador jokes in response as he joins Mel. 'We live quite the divine existence. Lucky for us we're up here where we belong and not down there with *those* people,' he says, screwing up his nose.

Mel looks on in silence. What exactly did he mean by that? She shrugs it off. Salvador's not a mean guy, he's just a fun-loving person who wants everyone to join in on the adventures.

Lauren walks towards them, carrying something in

her arms. 'Who wants to cuddle Puglet?' She holds the blanket-wrapped bundle out towards Salvador. A moment later, a tiny pig's snout pops up.

'Oh my god, that's the cutest thing ever!' Mel squeals in surprise, leaning in to scratch the pig on the head, cooing at it like it's a baby.

'Puglet! Come to Uncle Salvador, that's a good piggy.' Salvador gently scoops up the blanket and puts Puglet's snout on Mel's face. 'Give Pineapple a kiss.'

'It tickles!' Mel laughs. She's met people with pigs before, but they live on farms, not in a Hollywood mansion! She turns to Lauren. 'So, you own this house?' Mel didn't realise that being in a band could get you *this* much money. She's always reading stories about struggling artists having to work two jobs as well as doing their music. Things must be different in America.

Lauren shakes her head. 'No, I live with –' Just then, Lauren spies somebody rolling out a cart full of golf clubs, clearly intending to whack golf balls over the cliff. 'Hey!' she calls to the group of guys, turning away from Mel. 'Get your mitts off of them, my dad will crucify you!' She walks over and grabs the clubs out of their hands.

Mel realises this must be Lauren's family home. It's funny, a lot of Double Denim's songs are about simple coastal living and doing it tough. It seems entirely out of place for Lauren to be here.

Her tummy gurgles, begging her to find food. A group of people at the pool strip off and push each other in, still holding their cups in the air.

'Hey, do you know where the pizza is?' Mel calls to them, staying back from the edge for fear she'll be dragged in.

'It's thatta way, in the house,' says a guy who's wearing just his underwear and sunglasses, cowering as a group of girls splash him. 'Hop in, join us.'

Mel shakes her head. 'Isn't it cold?'

'Not when you're wasted!' They all giggle and the guy turns and starts making out with the girl next to him. It's a bit ick, so Mel walks away.

She almost weeps with delight when she sees a dozen pizza boxes spread across the table in culinary chaos. Among the mess of lone crusts and half-eaten slices, Mel spies an entire pizza that's yet to be tampered with. She moves the box to the side of the table, hoping for a moment alone in food heaven. She works her first slice free and it's so enormous, she needs two hands to hold it. She lifts it up and guides the pointy end into her mouth, relishing the hit of melted cheese and black olives.

'Pineapple! Bring that pizza hither! The Salvies are famished!'

Mel turns only her head, her body language defending the pizza. Salvador is sprawled on a large daybed surrounded by Susie, Tiffany, Lauren and a few other girls. Mel laughs and holds a finger in the air, telling him to wait. She dives in for another slice and holds it in her mouth as she carries two boxes over to where they're sitting.

'Mmmm,' she drools, handing the pizzas over and taking a bite of the one in her mouth. 'They're so much bigger than the slices at home, I think I'm done.'

'Darling,' Salvador says, eating messily and adding tomato stains to the drink already spilled down the front of his shirt. '*Everything's* bigger in America: burgers, bellies, bank balances ... egos,' he says, pausing, then bursting out in hysterical laughter. 'Come, come.'

Mel grabs a cushion and sits against it on the daybed, and they watch the party build into a frenzy. A young woman with short pink-streaked blonde hair and a studded black singlet is behind the DJ decks, pulling back the music and then dropping into the muddy fuzzed-out bass of dubstep.

'Woo, yeah, Tazer,' Salvador screeches. 'Tazer's one of the hottest DJs on the planet,' he says to Mel, closing his eyes, holding up his cup and nodding his head to the music. 'She was personally asked to play at Taylor Swift's party last month, but declined because it didn't fit her brand. How *Hollywood* of her! "Sorry Tay Tay but you're just a bit blah!"' he says in a mocking tone.

Mel laughs, trying not to show that she quite likes Taylor Swift. When they were younger she and Jaspa used to make up dance routines to 'Shake It Off', which they would perform to Jaspa's parents. Mel always insisted on taking the lead while Jaspa was back-up.

'Speaking of blah,' Salvador sits up and scans the room, 'where are all the hot, hot, hotties at this damn party, Lauren?'

'Well, not everyone can be as beautifully blessed as us, Salvador,' Lauren says, tapping a cigarette out of the packet, placing it between her teeth and lighting it. She offers the packet to Mel, who shakes her head.

'No thanks, I've given up.' By 'given up' she means she tried it once or twice and hates it.

'You're quite the goodie wholesome girl, aren't you, Pineapple?' Salvador says with a hint of snarkiness Mel hadn't detected before. 'No drinking, no smoking. So what kind of fun *do* you want to get up to tonight, hmmm?'

Mel fidgets, rubbing her thumb and forefinger together. 'I kinda should be going home soon, if that's cool?'

'Yes, yes, don't worry about that,' Salvador dismisses her with a wave. 'So, what about your love or lust life? Do you have someone special back in outback land?'

'Nah, just, you know, the guys are a bit boring at home. I'm waiting for someone phenomenal.'

'Oh.' Salvador sticks out his bottom lip and fakes sympathy while glancing between Susie, Tiffany and Lauren. 'She wants something phenomenal, how adorably teenage.'

Mel frowns. *But they're teenagers, too?* Older, yes, but still teenagers.

'Maybe Mr Phenomenal is right here. Scoot over. Let's play hot or not.' Salvador pushes the other girls away with his legs so Mel can come in closer. He points to various people, in the house, on the balcony, around the pool, and asks Mel if she thinks they're hot or not. At first it's fun, but then it turns mean as Salvador and the others start giving people horrible nicknames, like pug nose and flab guts.

Mel spies Corey across the yard talking to a group of people. He waves, and she responds by wriggling her fingers in the air, blushing as she stares at him.

'Oh, shut the front door, you like Corey!' Salvador says, giving Susie and Lauren a discreet elbow jab behind Mel's back.

'Well …' Mel begins, dropping her head with a grin, suddenly feeling uncharacteristically shy.

'Honey, you should go for it,' Susie says, trying to keep a straight face.

'He actually told me he's super into you,' Lauren jumps in.

'Pineapple, I think you know what needs to be done.' Salvador slaps the other girls behind him as they contain their snickers into each other's shoulders. 'Get over there and show him what your sun-kissed lips are made of.'

#23

Mel slowly gets up and makes her way over to Corey. She glances back at Salvador and the girls for support, and sees that they're laughing hysterically. When they see her looking, they immediately stop and give her encouraging smiles, waving for her to keep going. As she gets nearer she realises she hasn't even thought about how she should play this. Does she dive right in, or wait for him to make the first move? He's been pretty slow at reading the signs so far. Her face warms, and nerves flutter from the pit of her stomach to the top of her chest. The people around Corey slowly break away and he's suddenly alone, dunking chips into dip and popping them into his mouth. Mel secretly hopes it isn't full of onion or garlic.

'Hey,' she says, approaching the wall he's leaning against. 'Watcha looking at?'

'That,' he says, stepping back and guiding Mel to stand on the other side of him.

'Jesus!' Mel gasps. 'I can't believe it's right *there.*' Around the side of the house and up the hill is the Hollywood sign, its illuminated white letters hovering on a blacked-out backdrop of mountain and sky. She takes out her phone and ushers Corey in for a selfie. They linger, well after the photo has been taken, his warm breath skimming across her cheekbone and his lips inches from her skin. She feels giddy at how perfect this is. She carefully slips her phone back into her pocket, not wanting to move. Her eyes close and she tilts her face towards Corey, then slightly parts her mouth onto his bottom lip. The moment is cosy and tender, so she leans into the kiss.

'Hey, what are you doing?' Corey pushes back and wipes his mouth with his sleeve. 'I have a boyfriend, I thought you knew that?'

Mel is stunned. Boyfriend? She looks past him to see Salvador and the girls falling over themselves with laughter. Her head hangs as she begins to process the situation. She is mortified. Embarrassment is not something that readily affects Mel, but right now it creeps right through her. And it's suffocating.

'I'm, I'm … sorry. I didn't know.' As Mel scurries away, desperate to escape, a boy strides up to Corey and slips an arm around his waist.

'What was that all about?'

'Oh, you know,' Corey says, turning to his partner, 'just a little girl with silly dreams.'

Mel pushes through the bathroom door and slams it behind her, then turns to fumble with the lock. She whacks the heel of her hand into her forehead. How could she be so stupid? And why did the others tell her to go for it? Her mind scatters as she realises that Salvador and his stupid Salvies were all being mean. She thought they were cool. She thought they were her friends.

The excitement of the limo, the concert, the VIP platform and the afterparty has worn off, and her stomach is starting to churn. She pulls out her phone and dread pours over her like a tonne of cement. It's past midnight. *Crap. CRAP!* Tears flood Mel's eyes and she momentarily succumbs to her emotions, sobbing hopelessly into her hands. She wishes she was back in Malibu, safely asleep in her room with Jaspa and Carolyn. Her friends.

Slumping over the sink, she dry retches, then rinses her mouth and splashes cold water onto her face. Water drips down her top as she straightens and studies her reflection in the mirror. A look of fear has crept into her eyes. She lowers herself down to sit against the wall. The tiles are cold, so she reaches for the fluffy apricot bath mat and shuffles it under her bum, then pulls her knees to her chest and lowers her head.

A banging on the door wakes her with a start. *Jesus!* Dread washes over her as she realises where she is. *How long have I been asleep?*

'Just a minute,' she snaps.

'Hurry up, I'm going to chuck all over this floor,' says an angry voice from outside.

Mel releases a deep sigh and gets to her feet. She slips her bag over her shoulder and smooths down her hair with her hand, realising that at some point she's lost Carolyn's hat and her jacket.

When Mel opens the bathroom door, a girl she's never met before turns to her friend and snorts. 'Oh look, it's Corey's little girlfriend.' They push past Mel, snickering and stumbling as one girl hurls into the sink.

Mel clenches her teeth, sucks air into her nostrils and holds her breath for a moment. People are still dancing, only now it's more of a stumble, and several people are curled up on the furniture. Mel walks across the patio to Salvador and the others, who are still on the daybed, but now contorted into various sleeping positions. Salvador's on his back, his mouth gaping. His snore rumbles as Mel draws nears. She bends down to shake his foot.

'Hey. Salvador, wake up,' she whispers.

He groans and mumbles something incoherent, then turns over.

'Hey,' Mel says a little louder. 'Please wake up, I need to get home.'

'Don't stress, little pineapple head, we'll go in the morning.'

'No, I need to go now!'

'Listen,' Salvador half opens his eyes and slurs his words, 'I am way too wasted for this conversation. I did not sign up to be a babysitter.' He rolls over to face the other way, and resumes snoring.

Mel's heart races with a mix of anger and dread. What now? She walks to the far end of the pool and sits on a sunlounge, then texts Jaspa.

Jazz I'm still out and can't get home. Don't even know exactly where I am. It's Lauren's house in the hills. I've had a crappy night and just want to get back. Can you stall Thommo for me? xx

#24

Jaspa rolls over and pulls the doona tight around her as her eyes slowly flutter awake. A soft darkness still lies beyond the curtains, but the birds have started to stir the rest of the world awake. She rubs the corners of her eyes, then freezes, her heart giving an enormous thump. Bolting upright, she squints over to see that Mel's bed is still empty. Panic floods her body as she frantically scuffs around in the sheets, trying to remember where she put her phone. She grabs her coat and fishes it out of her pocket, then reads the message from Mel. Her eyes widen and she stares straight ahead, almost forgetting to breathe.

'Carolyn,' she whispers across the darkened room. 'Carolyn!'

'Huh? What?' Carolyn props up on her forearms

and looks at Jaspa, bleary-eyed, with her curly hair sprouting in different directions.

Jaspa points towards Mel's bed.

'Oh dude, no way.' She sits up and comes over to Jaspa's bed. 'What's the deal?'

'This.' Jaspa hands Carolyn her phone. 'I don't know what to do. What should we do?'

Carolyn studies the message then looks up. 'I guess we just have to stall Mr Sampson until she gets back.'

Jaspa's mouth quivers. 'I've got my semi final today.'

Carolyn slumps. 'Dammit, of course. Umm.' She jiggles her leg up and down while she thinks. 'Cooper's taking you for a surf training sesh at sunrise, yeah?'

Jaspa wipes the tears from her face and nods.

'And Mr Sampson knows you and Cooper are getting up early to do that?'

Jaspa sniffs into a tissue. 'Yes. He's meeting us at the comp around eight-thirty to find out if it's on or not.'

Carolyn shuffles in closer to Jaspa and pats her knee awkwardly. She's never been good at comforting others or showing affection. 'Cool, well here's what we'll do. I'll stay here to guard the bedroom and we'll text each other and work it out once we hear from Mel. Okay?'

'Okay, I guess.' Jaspa gets up and starts packing her daypack when a knock at the door startles them both.

Carolyn leaps across the bed and opens the door an inch.

'Oh, it's just Cooper,' she whispers behind her. 'Head downstairs, Jaspa will be out in a minute.' Carolyn eases the door closed and then turns to Jaspa. 'Yo, don't stress about it. You know what Mel's like, she's tough as. She's probs partying her guts out.'

Jaspa bites her lip. 'She didn't sound very tough in her text. She sounded scared.'

Jaspa and Cooper show their security passes to the guard and walk up the stairs to the competition deck. It's deserted. None of the lights have been turned on yet and the sun's only just started to yawn its way over the mountains. The sky is a stunning wisp of dark purple and orange, and Jaspa can just make out lines of white-water peeling down from the point. As she prepares to change into her wetsuit she feels her phone vibrating in her backpack.

'Mel,' she says, dropping her board and bag. 'Mel, where are you, are you okay?'

'I'm, I'm ...'

There's a silence, and Jaspa can tell Mel's struggling to compose herself.

'Everyone's still sleeping or out of it. I just wanna come home, Jazz. They're being assholes. I don't know how to get home.'

Jaspa listens to Mel's sobs down the phone. She rests her elbow on her knee and drops her head into her hand. 'Mel, where are you, what's the address? Should I get Mr Sampson?'

'No! Don't tell him ye—'

The phone goes silent. Jaspa holds it up, punching the on button, then realises she forgot to put it on charge last night. Her breath becomes stilted as she tries to contain her tears.

Cooper rushes over. 'Hey, hey, what's the matter, Jazz?' Just as he sits down and cups her into his side, stroking her hair, someone walks in.

'Heck, sorry.' Gloria Cruz pauses at the door, her surfboard under one arm and a wetsuit and towel draped over her shoulder. 'I didn't expect anyone else to be here.'

Jaspa looks up and smiles weakly.

'Is, err, is everything okay?' Gloria asks awkwardly without making eye contact.

Jaspa uses the cuff of her coat to wipe her face. 'It's my friend, Mel,' she says.

Gloria grunts at the name, but Jaspa continues on, oblivious. 'She's somewhere lost in the Hollywood Hills at that Lauren girl's house, and she can't get home and she's really scared and I think people are being mean to her and our teacher doesn't know and she wants me to keep it from him, and,' she runs out of air and takes a deep breath, then collapses into sobs.

Gloria rolls her eyes and releases an exaggerated sigh. She didn't sign up for this. 'Come on,' she says, gesturing for Jaspa and Cooper to get up. 'I'll take you.'

'What?' Jaspa blinks, her lashes wet and sticky around her blue saucer-shaped eyes. 'You will?'

'Yep. Unless you don't hurry up and I change my damn mind.'

#25

Mel is sitting on the sun lounge, hanging her head between her knees. It's 6.30 am and she's still no closer to knowing how she's going to get back to Malibu. She barely managed two hours sleep last night. Her mind is groggy but she waits, hoping she'll have a brainwave about what she should do next. She hopes Jaspa can hold Mr Sampson off for a little bit longer, but every time she tries to call her it goes straight to voicemail. She feels like a whimpering dog that burrowed under the gate and went off on an adventure, but ran too far and can't find its way home.

A group of people walk towards her, headed for the driveway.

'Hey,' Mel jolts up, thinking she might be in luck. 'Are you going anywhere near Malibu?'

'Oh, no, sorry honey,' one of the girls draws out, leaning clumsily against her boyfriend. 'Our car's, like, totally packed. Why don't you ask Corey?'

They disappear down the stairs, their laughter echoing behind them. Mel drops her gaze to hide her tears, wishing she'd never tried to kiss Corey. What was she thinking?

Suddenly she hears her name being called. She swings around to see Jaspa run across the patio and launch onto the sun lounge to embrace her. As they cry into each other's shoulders, Cooper comes over to join them. Gloria storms past, looks around the garden, then stops at the daybed where Salvador, Corey, Susie and Lauren are all in a deep sleep. Gloria lifts her foot and slams it into Salvador's leg. 'Hey, wake up!' He doesn't stir, so she kicks him again with twice the force. 'Wake the hell up, you piece of shit.'

Salvador's eyes flicker open. 'Gloria?' he says, holding up his arm to shield his eyes from the early morning light. 'What are you doing here, did they release you from the ghetto?'

Gloria grabs his arm and twists it, ignoring his protests. 'You freakin' led a fifteen-year-old girl astray and scared her senseless.' She lets go of his arm and points at the others, one by one. 'I hope you all drown in a puddle of your own self-entitled scum.' Gloria strides back to where Mel, Jaspa and Cooper are gathered and barks, 'Come,' then heads down the stairs.

'What the hell is going on here?' Mel asks Jaspa with a puzzled expression.

'It's a long story, but Gloria brought us here. She basically saved you.'

As they pile into the hatchback, Gloria slams her hand against the steering wheel in frustration. *'Salvador eres un cerdo racista,'* she whispers, then starts the car and speeds down the driveway.

The car exits onto the road and heads towards Hollywood Boulevard. As they make their way back to Malibu in silence, Jaspa rests her head on Cooper's shoulder. The adrenaline and emotion of the rescue has worn off, leaving behind a cloud of tension.

From the passenger seat, Mel lifts her eyes towards Gloria. 'I agree he's a pig. But why is he racist?'

'Wait, you speak Spanish?' Gloria is staring straight ahead, her face blank.

'A little bit,' Mel says timidly. She still can't get her head around what's happened and how she ended up in Gloria Cruz's car. 'Do you mean he's racist to you? But aren't you Mexican as well?'

'*Si*, but he's especially racist to us, when we don't have no *dinero*. No money.'

'Oh.' Mel hangs her head. 'Sorry, I didn't know.'

'Don't feel sorry for me. I have a happy life with my mamma, my brothers and sister. I would rather be a poor me than a rich asshole.'

Mel sighs and looks out the window as the rest of the trip passes in silence. She spots a sign reading 'Beverly Hills' and her stomach turns, wondering if one of the surrounding mansions is Salvador's. The way they mocked her was so unexpected. How did she get them so wrong?

Gloria pulls up at the contest site. 'You guys get out here, I have to park.'

Mel unclips her seat belt, gets out and then leans down to thank Gloria. But before she can get the words out, Gloria zooms off. Mel pulls her hands away and jumps back. *Well, guess we'll never be friends.* She walks upstairs to the competitors' area to find Jaspa wetting her hair over the sink in the change room and combing it.

'What are you doing? You know you'll be getting your hair wet in the actual ocean soon, right?' Mel says, looking at a text from Carolyn that says she and Mr Sampson are on their way.

'Yes, I know. But Mr Sampson thinks I went training this morning,' Jaspa says sternly, combing her hair in the mirror without looking at Mel.

'Oh. Right.' Mel drops her gaze and picks up a top

from Jaspa's backpack. 'Can I borrow this? I need to look rugged-up and sick.'

'Yep.'

'Okay, so, see you in the main section soon? Thommo is on his way.'

'Yep.'

Mel slips on the top and drags a stool up to one of the tables. Is Jaspa pissed off at her? But why? All she did was come and get her. Or is it because she got to be backstage at a Double Denim concert? She shrugs. That's Jaspa's problem.

Carolyn and Thomas appear at the entrance and Mel's heart races. She spies the black VIP wristband poking out from beneath her sleeve, and quickly tucks it away.

'Melissa, good to see you're feeling better. Where's Jaspa? They're starting the semi finals in thirty minutes, girls first.'

Mel points towards the lockers, then waits until Thomas is out of sight before turning to Carolyn. 'Hey, thanks for covering for me. That was hectic.'

'Yep, you got that right,' Carolyn says.

'What did you tell Thommo this morning?'

'When you said you were on your way home he was outside training with the boys, so I just told him you'd gotten up and bailed to see Jaspa.'

'Jesus, thanks. So freakin' close. Shhh.' Mel widens her eyes at Carolyn as Thomas returns to the table.

'How's Jazz doing?' Mel asks him. 'Is she pumped?'

'She's okay. A little quiet, and tired.' He sits down.

Mel looks over at Jaspa, suited up and slowly rubbing wax over her board. 'I'll be back.' She gets up and walks over to intercept Jaspa at the stairs. 'Hey chick, just wanted to give you a big good luck hug.' Mel swings her arms around Jaspa, who stiffens under her touch. 'Love you,' Mel says as they break apart.

'Thanks,' Jaspa responds before retreating down the stairs without turning back.

Mel pauses for a moment, processing the distance that's appeared between them. Usually it's Mel giving Jaspa the cold shoulder when they fight. Jaspa's the chirpy, shiny, perker-upper, not the other way around.

Mel joins the coffee queue, tucking a strand of hair behind her ear, then remembers Carolyn's hat. *Dammit.* She'll have to tell her. There's no way she'll be getting crowned Friend of the Year.

Mel carries three drinks back to Carolyn and Thomas. 'Check out these mad skills,' she says, resting a triangle of cups between her thumb and fingers.

'Thank you. What's that?' Thomas asks, pointing to Mel's wrist.

Mel looks down at the black band with 'Double

Denim After Party' written on it in white. *Oh crap.* She glances at Carolyn, who stares straight back at her with a stunned smirk, eager to see where this conversation goes. 'Oh, this? I err, I,' Mel slowly shuffles onto her stool and takes a sip of hot chocolate to stall. 'Some friends gave it to me. Yesterday, before my heat.'

'Friends?' Thomas asks.

'Yeah,' she says into her cup. 'Just some people I met around the contest site. I think it's the name of a new song or something.'

'Your friends' new song?' Thomas asks without flinching.

'Yeah. No,' she corrects herself. 'The band, Double Denim. They know I like the band. The friends.' Mel sees Jaspa paddling out. 'Look, Jazz's first wave,' she says, pointing at the ocean in a desperate bid to end this conversation.

Mel grimaces as Jaspa falls on her first ride. The swell has risen, and the waves are lining up and wrapping onto the bank, providing an uninterrupted canvas to carve upon. These conditions suit Jaspa's swooping style and flawless transitions perfectly, but something's not right. Mel watches, nervously tapping her foot on the stool. Jaspa seems uncharacteristically out of synch with the ocean, moving sluggishly to her feet, mistiming manoeuvres, getting caught behind sections. Mel leans back and sighs at the ceiling as the siren sounds and the announcer calls that Jaspa is last in fourth place.

Mel hurries downstairs and runs across the sand to Jaspa, who storms straight past her without a word.

#26

'Hey, what are you doing?' Mel asks, trying to keep up as Jaspa strides to the competition area.

'I don't want to talk to you,' Jaspa says without turning, using her height advantage to increase her pace.

'What? Why?' Mel asks. She reaches out for Jaspa's elbow, but her friend whips it away. 'Jaspa, stop!'

'Mel,' Jaspa swings around, her mouth quivering and her eyes wet. 'I didn't want to do this here, but since you keep insisting, fine. I just can't believe what you did. You skipped my quarter final yesterday – your best friend's quarter final – just so you could run off with your new rich mates, and then you put me in a position where I have to lie, like, over and over, to Mr Sampson, and you know I hate lying, and the whole time we've been here you've been going on about how boring our home is and how fun and famous your new friends are, and if you're wondering why Gloria doesn't like you, well that's why, and I have to say I agree with her, and you barely even thanked us for rescuing you, and you didn't even ask how Tyler went in his heat, do you even remember or care that he almost died last year? And I just want to know when my best friend since forever became so horribly selfish and materialistic.' She draws in a deep breath and chokes back her sobs.

Mel stands fixed to the sand, her mouth gaping as Cooper brushes past her and puts a towel around Jaspa's shoulders. 'Why don't you just give her a minute,' he says gently to Mel as he guides Jaspa away.

Mel is overcome by a wave of nausea and her heart feels like it's been physically twisted. She's been so caught up in chasing what she thought was her dream, she completely dogged the people she cares about the most.

'Are you okay?' asks a voice from behind her.

Mel turns to see Wil standing awkwardly with his hands in his pockets. 'Oh hey, hi. Did you just hear all that?' she asks.

'I did. Sorry, I wasn't, like, stalking or anything, but yeah, I heard.' He reaches out and squeezes her shoulder. 'So, are you okay?'

'Except for the fact that I've been a total bitch, yeah, just great.' Shame ripples through Mel like a river. She hasn't exactly been pleasant to Wil either, yet here he is being nice to her. His hand remains on her shoulder and she doesn't even push it away. His touch is warm and genuine. He draws her in close and strokes the back of her head. She bristles – this is too much, too intimate. Guys are usually drawn to her because she's fun and outrageous, not because she's vulnerable.

Her shoulders stiffen and she breaks away. 'Okay, well thanks. I'd better get going.' She turns and leaves without making eye contact. Halfway up the stairs, she spies Jaspa sitting alone on a rock a few feet away with her head down. Mel hesitates, wondering if she should leave her for a little longer. But this is Jaspa. They've been best friends for almost ten years. Mel has spent practically the same amount of time sleeping at Jaspa's house as she has in her own bed, and when Jaspa's brother, Tyler, went missing last year Mel didn't leave her side.

Before she knows it, Mel is standing right in front of Jaspa.

'Hey, can we talk?' Mel fiddles with a loose thread on the hem of her top.

'Well,' Jaspa says, getting to her feet, 'I guess we

have to at some point. Better now than in front of everyone back at the house.'

Mel suggests that they take a walk up the beach. 'You were right, about everything,' she says as they leave the noise of the contest site behind them. 'You know I love an adventure, but I got out of hand.'

'It's like you can never accept something to be just plain and normal,' Jaspa says, bending down to pick up a shell.

Mel frowns. 'I'm not going to apologise for that, Jazz. I don't want to be normal!'

Jaspa glances sideways at Mel. 'That came out wrong. What I mean is, you can't just sit still and *be*. You're always searching for something to be next level.'

Mel grabs Jaspa's arm, pulling her to a stop. 'But Jazz, that's just me. I'm not calm and collected like you. I'm busting with energy I have to unleash, and that sometimes gets me into a bit of trouble.' She takes off her sunglasses and looks directly at Jaspa. 'But that also means I push us into bigger waves. It's why we decided to try and qualify for the tour. Heck, my bluntness is how we started the Bikini Collective. But you're right, I shouldn't have ditched you for the others, and I shouldn't have asked you to lie for me.'

They sit down cross-legged on a patch of grass. 'You're right,' Jaspa says, twirling the shell in her fingers.

'I wouldn't be with Cooper if it wasn't for you pushing us together.'

A hint of annoyance prickles up Mel's back. 'Speaking of which,' Mel raises one knee and wraps her arms around it, 'it's not that I don't like Cooper, you know I do, he's a good guy. But you're with him *all* the time. I've gone from having a best friend who I see every day to being lucky if we hang out once a week. It gets lonely.'

'I —' Jaspa sucks in her cheeks to ward off the tears. 'I'm so, so sorry, Mel. I didn't even consider that. How could I have let that happen?' Jaspa hangs her head.

'Look, the most important thing is, we've got a killer friendship. Maybe our differences are what make it so spesh,' Mel says.

Jaspa wipes her face and rests her head on Mel's shoulder as they look out to sea and cheer Gloria on as she prepares for the final.

'Where should I pop these?' Mel asks Trudy, peering out from behind the stack of boxes she's carrying. Now that the contest is over, they can use the site for the Bikini Collective Ocean Play Day. Mel can't believe how much Trudy has helped them. She got a big The Bikini Collective banner made, which they're allowed to take home after the event. All of the sponsors donated door prizes and sample goodies. The local surf school is assisting with boards, wetsuits and even instructors, and the Santa Monica Arts College has provided Carolyn with a bunch of supplies for her painting class.

'Just on that table over there,' Trudy calls from the top of a stepladder as she ties the banner to the gazebo. 'Everything's already sorted into prize packs, so you only have to open the boxes.'

'Sweet,' Mel says. 'That's it, everything's ready. And, look, people are starting to arrive.' She points towards the car park.

Jaspa directs the participants to the registration desk, where they fill out some forms, then Mel ushers them over to sit on the floor while the adults stand to the side.

Mel looks at her watch and asks Trudy, 'Right, time to start?'

Trudy nods and sits down next to Gloria and southern Californian surfer Nikki James.

'Okay,' Mel claps her hands to quieten the crowd. 'Hello everyone, we'd like to offer you a big, salty, heartfelt welcome to the Bikini Collective Ocean Play Day! Are you excited?' An enthusiastic chorus of 'yes' comes from the floor. 'Today is all about having fun and supporting each other, no matter what ocean activity you choose to do. First off we're going to have a Q and A with these amazing surfers. We have three-time World Champion Trudy Hardwick, Gloria Cruz, who just yesterday won the Malibu Pro Junior, and last year's World Junior Champion, Nikki James. And I'm Mel. I started The Bikini Collective with my best friends Jaspa and Carolyn,' she says, pointing to the girls. 'So who would like to ask the first question?'

Girls giggle and hang their heads shyly, waiting to

see who will speak first. A girl in the second row with a face dotted with freckles raises her hand. 'Hi there, tell us your name and your question,' Mel says.

'My name's Evie, I'm eleven, and I want to know what we should do if boys tell us we can't be surfers.'

'You can tell them the ocean's for absolutely everyone and that girls have the right to try anything they like, especially surfing,' Trudy says.

'And then you get out there and show 'em how it's done,' Gloria adds.

Mel points to a girl whose hand shoots up from the centre of the group. 'I'm thirteen, my name's Sasha and I want to know where you live and what it's like,' she asks, pointing to Mel.

'Us three are from Australia. Jaspa and I live in a small town called Bonita Shores, and it's very quiet, and it's, it's ... it's extremely beautiful, with amazing surf and lots of nature. I love it and I count myself very lucky to live there,' Mel says, squeezing Jaspa's hand. Questions dart from around the room, and each surfer takes a turn in delivering the answers.

'You, in the back,' Mel says, pointing to a girl who's using her hand to prop up her arm as it tires from being raised for so long. 'Lucky last goes to you.'

'I'm Olivia, I'm eight and my question is, what's it like to ride on a wave?'

All of the panel smile and nod their heads. 'It's like, you're totally in the moment,' Jaspa says. 'No other thoughts enter your head other than the journey you're on with that wave. And you glide, and dance along its surface, and sometimes they're fun and sometimes they scare you, but it's the most rewarding thing you'll ever do.'

'Goodie, I wanna do it!' Olivia responds with a clap.

'Well then, how about we get out there?' Mel says, and the crowd squeals 'yes!'

'Those who want to do some surf art, head to the next tent with Carolyn. The rest of you can come and collect your boards and wetsuits.' As Mel treks back and forth up the beach, carrying the equipment to the shore, she spots a familiar figure walking towards her.

'Hey,' Wil says, crinkling his nose to stare into the sun. 'We came down to help. What can we do?'

Mel looks behind Wil to see Thomas, Cooper and Tyler standing at the top tent. She smiles, and before her usual instinct to put up a wall kicks in, she reaches out and hooks her hand into his. 'Wil, you're a bloody legend.' She points to the pile of boards. 'All of those need leg-ropes attached, then they can be taken to the shore please. Hey,' Mel says as he begins to walk away.

He turns around, once again squinting his eyes, which Mel finds unexpectedly adorable. 'Yeah?'

'You know, you're pretty alright, Wil Sanders.'

She watches him go with a smile, and a hint of redness blushes her cheeks. She turns to join Trudy, Gloria and Jaspa, who are assisting the surf instructors in showing the girls where to stand on the board, how to pop up properly and ride the whitewater in, and discussing rips, currents and how to do an ocean conditions check.

'Right,' Mel claps at the shoreline. 'Who's ready to come with me?'

'I am!' shouts a little girl with fire-red curly hair. Her wetsuit is two sizes too big, and she's barely able to hold even the smallest board in her arms.

'Oh my god,' Mel whispers to Jaspa. 'Sign the adoption papers now, look how adorable she is.'

Mel walks over and bends down. 'And who might you be?'

'I'm Morgan, and I'm seven. I'm from Ventura.'

'Oh, I surfed there the other day,' Mel says, smiling.

'Your accent's funny,' Morgan says with a giggle.

'It is? So is yours,' Mel laughs. 'Okay, so are you ready to become a surfer?' She takes the board from Morgan and pops it under her arm.

'No!' Morgan says urgently. 'I want to carry it! I want to be a real surfer.'

Mel looks down at Morgan's determined face, her

pale skin smothered in zinc and her sunhat tied under her chin. 'How about we carry it together?' She lowers the board so Morgan can stretch her arm around the front while Mel carries the back. They walk towards the ocean, then Mel helps Morgan onto the board and steers her just past the shoreline. The ocean is gentle today, and Morgan squeals with delight each time she rides a wave on her belly. Memories flood back to Mel of when she and Jaspa were first learning at Bonita Shores. Once they stood up on their first wave that was it, they were hooked.

'Can we go just a teensy bit further this time? Don't worry, I can handle it,' Morgan says over the sound of rolling waves.

Mel grins. 'Okay, just a little bit further. How about you try to pop up on this one?'

Morgan nods excitedly and Mel guides her out to where the whitewater is first breaking, then swings her around. 'Are you ready? There's a perfect one coming if you want it?'

'Yes!' Morgan screams. 'I was born ready!'

Mel gives the board a gentle push and watches the wave pick Morgan up and thrust her towards the beach. 'Right, now put your back leg in position and pop up!' She strides through the water to follow Morgan to the shore and watches her place her hands on the deck, drag up her back leg and then pop onto her front foot. 'Yes!' Mel calls, as Morgan rides with a wide stance, arms outstretched, her face etched with concentration.

'I did it, I did it!' Morgan beams, jumping from the board into the shallows, her sunhat slipping down to reveal her wet bouncy curls. 'I'm a real surfer now, just like you.' She throws herself at Mel, embracing her legs. 'That was the best feeling in the entire world. I never want it to end!'

Mel gently places one hand around Morgan's back, using the other to ruffle her hair. 'Me neither, grommet. Me neither.'

Your surf speak glossary!

a-frame a wave peak that peels both left and right.

backside/backhand riding a wave with your back to the ocean.

backwash when water pushes from the shore back towards a regular breaking wave, causing them to collide.

barrel/tube the hollow part of a breaking wave, which surfers can ride inside of, completely hidden from a shore view.

beach break waves that break over sand.

bottom turn generally the first turn you do, performed at the bottom of the wave.

closeout a wave that shuts down without peeling left or right.

cutback a turn you do on the open face to position yourself back near the critical pocket of the wave.

deck the side of the surfboard you lie down on.

drop the ride when you take off on a wave with the pitching lip.

duckdive pushing your board underneath a breaking a wave so you can pop out the other side.

face the 'green' smooth part of a breaking wave that isn't the whitewater.

floater a manoeuvre that involves gliding over the whitewater, usually so you can reach the open face or finish a ride.

frontside/forehand riding a wave facing the ocean.

glassy/glass-off when there is little to no wind and the ocean is smooth like a mirror.

goofy footer a surfer who stands on a board with their right foot forward. (The same term is also used for skateboarding and snowboarding.)

grommet/grom a young kid who surfs.

Huey the surfing god.

impact zone a spot in the line-up where the waves are breaking with the most power (don't get caught there!).

inside the position that's closest to the breaking pocket of the wave, where you have priority to take off over any other surfer. (The term 'caught on the inside' is also used when you're stuck in the impact zone.)

interference when a competitor drops in or obstructs the path of the surfer who has right of wave. The penalty is usually removal of the interferer's highest score.

kook/gumby a derogatory term used to describe someone who isn't a very good surfer.

layback a forehand manoeuvre where you end a turn by laying your back close to the water. A very '70s-style move.

left-hander a wave that peels left from the viewpoint of the surfer on the wave.

leg-rope the leash that attaches to your surfboard, which is wrapped around the ankle on your back leg.

line-up a position in the ocean where waves are breaking and the surfers are sitting.

lip the first point of a wave that pitches over. The lip can vary in intensity, from throwing with force to form a barrel, to crumbling along the face.

lull the time between sets when no waves are breaking.

natural footer a surfer who stands on a board with their left foot forward. (The same term is also used for skateboarding and snowboarding.)

offshore wind a wind blowing from the land onto the water, which makes the ocean nice and smooth.

ollie getting air by hopping the front of the board out of the water.

onshore wind a wind blowing from the ocean onto the land, making the ocean bumpy and sometimes tricky to surf.

outside a position that's on the other side of the surfer who's closest to the breaking pocket of the wave. When you're there you have to give way to the inside surfer, unless they encourage you to 'GO!'

out the back the furthest out to sea you can be, on the

other side of the breaking whitewater, while still in a position to catch waves.

overhead when you're riding a wave and its face is taller than you are.

over the falls when you take off but don't get to your feet, and fall with the pitching lip. Wipeout!

peak the point of a wave that pitches up, ready to break.

pop-up jumping to your feet on the take-off – the quicker, the better!

pull in what you do when you see a tube/barrel forming before you.

quiver collective noun for surfboards.

rail the edges around the sides of a surfboard, which you ideally want to carve deep into the water on your turns.

reef break a wave that breaks over reef – sometimes dead coral, sometimes alive. Be careful of your feet!

right-hander a wave that peels right from the viewpoint of the surfer on the wave.

roundtail when the tail of a surfboard is rounded – often preferred for barrelling waves.

re-entry (reo) a manoeuvre where you soar vertically into the top pocket of the wave and snap the board around underneath you.

set a group of waves that are usually bigger than the average on the day.

shaper someone who makes surfboards.

soul arch when you're on a wave and you stand stylishly still and tall for a moment with your back arched, old-school style!

squaretail when the tail of a surfboard is squared off at the end.

swallowtail a v-shape cut out of the tail of a surfboard.

take-off the moment you stop paddling for a wave and stand on your surfboard.

wipeout ooops, you've fallen off the wave!

The
Bikini
Collective
Book 1: Ocean Rules
By Kate McMahon

Three friends discover, surfing just got serious

What does it take to be the best, and what does that even *mean* anyway? Fifteen-year-old Jaspa Ryder is on the crest of qualifying to join surfing's prestigious World Junior Tour along with her best friends, Mel and Carolyn.

But as the girls soon discover, the ride to stardom doesn't come easy. Jaspa's head and heart are in battle – she isn't sure she *wants* to be a professional surfer, which, given her incredible talent, infuriates everyone, especially her envious brother. Who will qualify for the tour?

Will Jaspa's friendships survive the pressure of competition? Sometimes in life, you just have to jump to your feet, take off, and hope you don't wipe out.

> *"I felt utterly invested in Jaspa, Mel and Carolyn's surfing journey; can we be friends?"* **Stephanie Gilmore**
> *"A book that gets to the heart of surfing friendships and competition. A must-read for all young ocean lovers."* **Layne Beachley**

The
Bikini
Collective
Book 3: Sea of Gratitude
by Kate McMahon

Book three in *the Bikini Collective* series sees the girls preparing for another action-packed surfing adventure, but one of them is burdened with secrets. With all of her scholarship funds exhausted, Carolyn has no choice: she'll have to drop off the World Junior Tour. Just as all seems lost, the Bikini Collective – along with a mysterious donor – save the day. Next stop: Brazil!

The lush South American tropics are dreamy; playful waves, everyday fiestas and beautiful, smooth-talking Brazilians. But can Carolyn find what it means to truly be happy? Just like a calm ocean with a deceiving undercurrent, things aren't always what they seem.

"McMahon picks you up and drops you into the ocean with her."
Stephanie Gilmore

"Inspiring. Blue Crush for a new generation." **Sean Doherty**